The EROTOFLUIDIC AGE

VINNIE TESLA

Circlet Press, Inc.
Cambridge, Massachusetts

The Erotofluidic Age
by Vinnie Tesla

Copyright © 2011 Vinnie Tesla
First paperback edition July 2015
ISBN 978-1-61390-142-7

Circlet Press, Inc.
39 Hurlbut Street
Cambridge, MA 02138

www.circlet.com

Table of Contents

The Ontological Engine,

or, The Modern Leda

It is imperative that I make this utterly clear from the start: my motives in the affair of Miss Pertwee were the very highest. Desire for personal gain, worldly fame for the name of Daedalus Tesla, or selfish pleasure of any sort were absent from my mind at all junctures. I hope that my setting down the bare facts of the case will suffice to clarify that the dreadful outcome which resulted arose despite the noblest intentions on my part and could never have been reasonably foreseen.

My troubles began when I had been a Fellow of ————— College, Cambridge, for several years. In retrospect, it is clear that I was already beginning to tire of the position. A considerable family income left me free of the need for remunerative work, but I had initially hoped, foolishly, that the storied intellects of that renowned College would prove a congenial atmosphere for the life of the mind. How comically naive that seems to me now!

The laboratory facilities with which the college had provided me were, I suppose, adequate in size, though my budget was laughably small, given the importance of the work I was doing.

Nonetheless, certain of my researches demanded rather more re-moteness from the prying eyes of the jealous and the small-minded than was afforded by my official accommodations. By great good for-tune, I had come to be aware of a disused storage attic in ————— House and had managed to assemble an entirely adequate facility there for my more sensitive researches, with very few people the wiser for it.

The eventful May afternoon I propose to describe was a Wednesday, and being so, Mrs. Mathilde Hargreaves, wife of the Head of the Col-lege, was providing me with her inimitable assistance for the day's re-searches—my most ambitious exploration of ontological forces to date.

With trembling fingers, she disrobed, eager as always to aid in the cause of Science. I guided her to the padded collection platform, placed the metal circlet—which I had designed to channel the energies she produced so copiously—upon her head, and strapped her, face down, to the cushioned stand.

Once I had selected a suitable birch bundle, we commenced with the day's activities. The flagellation, oftentimes the highlight of our Wednesday research sessions, was that day the merest prelude. I did not even bother to activate the collection circuit as I briskly brought her wriggling posterior to a pleasingly roseate glow.

Coming around her, I found that the exercise had brought colour to her face as well, her dark eyes now moist and sparkling. When I inquired whether she was ready for the next phase of our experiment, she nodded most avidly.

It was now time to test my newly-augmented Electrick Vibratorium. When I flipped the switch, a great throbbing hum suffused the room. Mrs. Hargreaves jumped and squirmed about despite the lack of contact. I reached between her limbs and she ground her pubis against my hand most avidly, bedewing my knuckles with the fluids of her ardour. I pressed the swollen labia apart, exposing her clitoris, and pressed the buzzing pad of the Vibratorium against it, eliciting a long groan of delight from the hot-blooded woman. With some little effort, I subdued her motions sufficiently to strap the Vibratorium in place and then took my place at the control panel I had assembled.

I activated the Amatory Capacitors, and a crackling noise filled the air. It joined in pleasing counterpoint to the Vibratorium's hum and Mrs. Hargreaves's groans and gasps as my Ontological Engine woke to life, powered by the trickle of Vital Energies she was emitting.

We were entering a phase of the project that demanded the utmost care and patience. I was purposing to embark on the harnessing of ontological forces on an unprecedented scale—any error could derail the undertaking or render it gravely perilous.

My ears were to guide my labours of this time as much as my eyes. As Mrs. Hargreaves' cries rose in pitch and volume, they were joined by an acceleration in the crackling from the Ontological Engine. I twisted a knob, cutting power to the Vibratorium, and a note of dismay entered Mrs. Hargreaves's voice.

"Oh, pray, Mr. Tesla! Do not pause—I was so very close!"

"All in good time, dear lady," I assured her. "The day is yet young."

Impatiently, she struggled with her bonds, striving to press herself more firmly against the Vibratorium. Whistling merrily, I once more looked over the Engine's connections and switches, the lusty woman's desperate moans sweet music to my ears.

Arrayed on the work-table before me was a divers array of exotic materials from the Americas, each singularly rich, according to my instruments, in Vital Fluid.

Long did I ply that dial, ever and again raising Mrs. Hargreaves's pleasure to the utmost, then denying her the release she so urgently craved, while the crackling of the Ontological Engine, and its unearthly blue glow, rose and fell with the lady's excitement.

"I think things may be nearly in readiness," I told the writhing woman at last, but the observation was met merely with gasps as she strove to regain her breath.

"Do you think you would like to spend now?" I inquired.

At this she found breath. "Oh, yes, yes! I cannot abide another moment of this abominable teasing!"

I had made something of a study of this woman's particular tastes, and I possessed a smattering of knowledge of how to maximize her excitement, and thus her output of Vital Fluids.

"Beg," I said coldly.

"Oh, pray, Mr. Tesla," she gasped, "I beg of you, allow me to spend. Oh, I crave it so! I shall be your servant in all things, if only you permit it!"

Not particularly ingenious, but one must make allowances for circumstance. Slowly, slowly, I began to turn the dial upward.

Moans gave way to cries, cries to shrieks. Much of my attention was consumed with adjustments to the Ontological Engine as I made ready to marshal its forces to best effect.

The moment of Mrs. Hargreaves's maximum pleasure came, and the room was suffused with a flickering blue light. I threw the switch. The Ontological Engine came fully to life, throwing its powers onto the arrayed materials. Small vortices of ontological energies formed, drifting away from the table before dissipating into the air. One struck a potted ficus by the window, which opened golden, slitted eyes and watched the proceedings intently; another brushed the sleeve of my coat, where good brown Irish tweed blushed a vulgar scarlet, turning to crushed velvet for a few seconds before fading to tweed once more.

My attention to these processes was interrupted by a splintering bang as the locked door to the storage room was forced open.

"Mathilde!" Professor Hargreaves's bellow was as unmistakable as it was unwelcome.

"Fear not, darling! I am here to rescue you!" he cried out.

On the work-table, my materials were merging, taking on new forms, new aspects. On the Collection Stand, Mrs. Hargreaves was still trembling violently against the Vibratorium; I suspect that her cries had covered the arrival of her spouse and would-be rescuer, such that she remained blissfully unaware of his arrival.

"As for you, Tesla, you foul beast," Hargreaves continued, gathering rhetorical momentum, "it's the gallows for you now! Criminal! Rapist!"

"Do you mind, Hargreaves?" I said. "I'm a bit busy at the moment. Could we perhaps discuss this at another time?"

Hargreaves was undeterred. "Charlatan!" he persisted. "Mountebank!"

I whirled on him in a fury. "You dare—?" I began. But the reckless oaf was charging me like a bull. Before I could defend myself from this unprovoked assault, he struck, and the two of us were tumbling against my control panel, bringing it to the ground with a monstrous clatter. Inertia carried us backward, until a cable caught my foot, and I went sprawling to the floor. Hargreaves, however, ran up against the work-table, his head falling into the beam of blue light cast upon it.

My frantic kicking at the cable that entangled me detached the engine from the amatory collector, and the light faded.

I stood, and ascertaining my parts to be largely undamaged, looked about. In the aftermath of the engine's radiance, I could make out naught but vague shapes in the storeroom's gloom. I strode to a window and threw open the blinds, allowing the daylight to stream in, revealing a tableau that shall remain always in my memory.

Nearest me, the ficus shielded its lambent eyes from the sudden glare with two furry grey paws, dragging itself away from the window with another four such.

On the Collection Stand, Mrs. Hargreaves had at last recovered sufficiently from her massive climax to become somewhat cognizant of the changes in her surroundings, constrained though she was by the straps that yet held her in place. "Augustus?" she said, looking in confusion at her husband.

For his part, he sat on the floor, mouth agape, feeling tentatively with his pudgy hands at the pair of incongruously handsome antlers which now sprouted proudly from his broad, gleaming forehead, rendering his marital status all too visible.

Beside him, on the work-table that had previously supported naught but my inert ingredients, three tiny creatures gurgled and squawked. Judging the day's experiment to be, if not complete, then at least terminated, I gathered the creatures on the work-table to my bosom and made my exit, leaving the Hargreaveses to discuss the day's events amongst themselves.

∽

Within a month of the incident, I had been removed from the faculty on grounds, according to the Deanery, of "gross immorality." I might say rather "failure to defer adequately to the bloated self-regard and withered, timid intellects of the college's Lords High Poo-Bah," but I grant that the former phrase is at least more concise and arresting.

The whole business was, to be sure, unfortunate, and not unmarked by errors of both analysis and judgment on my part. Nonetheless, Hargreaves had previously scoffed at my "ludicrous assertions" with regard to the power of ontological fields, and his fate had more than a whiff about it of poetic justice.

I rather fancy it was the validation of my theories which he had, in such extravagant and unequivocal terms, derided that rankled with him more than the more mundane humiliations attendant thereon.

I feel compelled to add that, in contrast to her husband's petty acrimony, Mrs. Hargreaves's refusal to press charges betrayed her own excellent breeding and fine character.

As for the other issue of my experiment, my feelings were even more mixed. My calculations had led me to believe that the outcome of the day's work might be some fabulous avatar of lasciviousness, mighty entities capable of—somehow—gathering ever-greater quantities of Vital Fluids, enabling ever-greater feats of ontological engineering.

Instead, at the end of the day's debacle, I was confronted with three mewling, gurgling wee creatures, patchily covered in fine down. Nonetheless, they were a concrete and exotic trophy of my mastery of ontological forces, and it seemed to me that they might well be of some practical value someday; though in what manner, I could scarce imagine.

Upon my ejection from the faculty, I had little choice but to return to the ancestral manse, and set about to remake myself, at least to the eyes of the world, as a reasonably unremarkable country squire, so as not to draw further unwelcome attention for my researches. My pets grew rapidly in the bracing country air, and, in less than a year, had reached nearly their ultimate proportions.

As they figure prominently in the tale before us, it would behoove me to describe them now. Webbed-footed, winged, and long-necked, their avian ancestry must needs be the first aspect that strikes any viewer. Another glance, however, and the impression is cast askew, for the body, neck, and head are not of any bird, but instead resemble that giant clam of the Pacific known as the "Geoduck." Their siphons, located where one might expect the bird's head and neck, serve for them as organs of consumption and generation, and despite the apparently featureless end, they hear and see adequately well, understanding speech better than any dog, and at least as well as several valets I can think of.

There is a third point of resemblance that bears noting. Those prehensile siphons, innocent of either hair of feathers, bear an arresting resemblance as well to, to put it indelicately, the biggest, most obscene and wrinkled, semi-tumescent male member imaginable.

Upon my return to Tesla Hall, I assembled as small a domestic staff as seemed consistent with my station in life, but found that, contrary to my fears, maintaining privacy in my affairs from them was no matter at all. To a one, my servants were loath to come near the door to my basement laboratory and were hugely reluctant to do so much as knock upon it, for fear, one supposes, of it coming to life and devouring them. Not that that was entirely outside the realm of possibility, come to think on it.

On the other hand, the forces I had available to work with were pitiably small. A massive coal-fired steam engine, imported at great cost from Liverpool, provided a modest trickle of ontological energies, but the conversions from heat to mechanical force to the ontological realm were heartbreakingly inefficient.

To the extent possible, I gave my ungainly little pets the run of the estate, and found that I had grown rather fond of the creatures. In time, they began taking a distinct interest in the female house servants, a warmth that was sadly unreciprocated, as the members of my staff were uniformly terrified of the harmless little dears.

My life thus proceeded rather drearily for many months as I moved in, made the minimal social rounds of the area, and worked to build a first class laboratory of ontological endeavour.

Then one day, a little more than a year after my taking up country life, I received a visit from a particularly talented former pupil of mine—one Victor Dalrymple, whose company I had always found quite reasonably congenial. He, for his part, was entirely unabashed about his admiration for my extraordinary intellectual accomplishments.

"My dear fellow!" he effused to me over our second bottle of sherry. "How aptly you match your namesake: master inventor and artificer!"

There was justice in his words, but the social niceties must be observed.

"Oh, you are too kind, Victor," I demurred. "I am naught but a woolly-headed theoretician. Why, even your mechanical skill is nearly a match for mine."

Victor seemed a bit taken aback by the extravagance of my praise. "Er... thank you," he said at last. Then he leaned in and spoke in hushed tones. "My dear fellow, I just want to you know that I consider the scurrilous charges old Hargreaves leveled against you to be libelous balderdash."

My surprise was unfeigned. "You do?"

"Daedalus, my friend. Anyone who knows you realizes that you are a man of science, not some sordid libertine rogue! Hargreaves is a spiteful ass, and his vague claims that you had 'disfigured' him were the most transparent poppycock. Why, if such a thing had occurred, why would he refuse to specify the nature of the damage done? Frankly, I am convinced that something was wrong with his head!"

I started guiltily. "Whatever do you mean?"

"Brain fever, old boy. The man is a bit cracked, to be blunt. Why, to this day, he refuses to remove his hat, even in church. It is quite the scandal about the old college."

He sat back and took another sip of his sherry. "Clearly, his jealousy of your brilliance eventually got the better of him, and he concocted his absurd fable to smear you!"

My eyes filled with tears at this speech, moved not merely by his display of faith in me, but by the poignant certainty that I could not, at that time, reveal to him the grain of truth in Hargreaves's malicious attacks, that my researches in pursuit of knowledge, in pursuit of human betterment, had once more served to isolate me, to sever me from the happy intercourse of the common run of man. For the first time in months, I was seized by the loneliness of the great, compounded by the prolonged isolation of my rural retreat.

To be a giant in a land of midgets is to be ineluctably isolated, and yet it occurred to me that some relief might be at hand, as well as solutions to certain other of my dilemmas.

"I say, Victor," I ventured, "I hope you will forgive the presumption. I well realize that such labour is vastly below your worldly station, but would you have any interest in assisting me at my researches?

"My dear friend," he said. "It would be a signal honour!"

The days that followed I still remember with distinct pleasure. Victor proved both an eager and an able assistant, turning his hand to tasks both difficult and menial with nearly equal ardour. We were, in many ways, a complimentary pair, my theoretical genius enhanced by his formidable mechanical ingenuity, his rosy complexion and bronze curls a contrast to my swarthier colouring, his buoyant naiveté a welcome tonic to my own bitter awareness of humanity's true nature. Withholding those aspects of my researches for which he was not yet prepared was an inconvenience, to be sure; and exposure to my full arsenal of equipment earned me a fair scattering of interrogative glances as he scrutinized the manacles, the electrodes, the Electrick Vibratorium. I urged him towards discretion as he went about in town, reminding him that there were those who would be eager to steal the secrets of ontological engineering to pervert it to their own selfish or immoral ends, and he pledged himself to perfect silence.

In time, he introduced me to the wonders that what other avenues of invention had recently been cast up into the world, arranging the installation of an Edison Electrick Tele-phone between my parlour and laboratory and bringing along his own collection of the latest modern Daguerreotype machines. Truly, it is an age of miracles in which we live!

Victor took wonderfully to the 'ducks, and they to him, nosing about him as he walked through the estate, following him in an orderly little line, poking their siphons inquisitively into every crevice of his constructions.

As our work advanced, he oversaw the purchase of an ever-larger and more modern series of steam engines, which, ravenous and temperamental consumers of coal though they were, proved modest indeed in their supplies of power. One day, in late March, I threw down my tools in frustration. "Dash this cursed temperamental steam engine!" I shouted. "This thing is filthy and inefficient, the coalman's bills are eating me alive, and its output is utterly inadequate to my purposes."

Victor was perplexed. "What source do you propose, then? Water? Wind?"

"Victor, dear friend, it is time to take you into my confidences. The energies that power the Ontological Engine are paltry when generated by mechanical force, but they are emitted copiously by human beings."

His puzzlement only deepened. "Would you have me operating a treadmill, then?"

"You misapprehend my purpose. The Vital Fluids that shall power the Ontological Engine are not the vulgar fruits of manual labor, but the finer emanations of the human spirit! Here. I believe a minor demonstration is in order. Help me prise open this crate."

We set to work with crowbars, and in a moment, we had unpacked the Amatory Condensers I had developed at Cambridge.

"Now, old fellow. Do you recall that one night at FitzSimmons Hall, after the servants had all gone to bed?"

Victor blushed to the roots of his hair. "I don't know what you... that is to say..."

I smiled. "You and Harry and Professor Lawrence and I had all had entirely too much of that excellent French brandy, and we were discussing zoology."

"I must have forgot—" Victor said.

"Now, now, Victor. You may have forgot, but it's clear your prick has not. It's standing out in your trousers quite proudly. Now do have it out and let me have a look."

Victor's hands clenched together in agitation, and he shifted uncomfortably from side to side. "I say, Daedalus. I mean, that sort of thing is quite all right when one is at University, but...."

"Out with it," I said more firmly.

Whether it was the lascivious memories I had summoned or the months of accustomed obedience to my orders, Victor tremblingly unfastened his breeches and drew out the handsome red cock I remembered so well.

I fell to my knees and took it into my mouth, the soft head swelling against my tongue as I began to exert suction upon it.

"Oh, Daedalus!" he cried, "I don't think I can— I believe I shall—"

"Excellent," I responded, frigging his gleaming length with one hand when he emerged from my mouth. "Be a good lad and don that circlet on the table there."

With a trembling hand, he took the metal band and rested it upon his head. At once a low hum began to emerge from the Ontological Engine, and a faint glow suffused it.

I stood. "Now I must ask you to attend to yourself while I attend to the engine." I guided his own hand to his rampant *dart of love* and manned the switches of the Ontological Engine.

On the work-table stood a crabapple from my own neglected orchards, a pair of categorical condensers trained upon it.

I adjusted the azimuth of materiality and disengaged the vitality stabilizers. To my side, Victor presented a wonderfully pleasing sight, his face darkly flushed, his handsome cock appearing and disappearing as he rapidly worked his hand upon it.

"I shall spend... I shall spend..." he whispered.

"Good. Behold!" I flipped the switch, and the engine's hum rose to a noisy whine. The Condensers cast the crabapple in an unearthly glow. The skin of the fruit swelled, coarsened, paled, till it had clearly become a grape-fruit. Victor groaned, and semen splattered across the work-table, a few drops hitting the grape-fruit, which sprouted eye stalks and four shaggy legs. The transformed crabapple blinked improbably long lashes at us as it looked about. Victor groaned and slumped, his spent cock softening in his hand. The glow of the condensers faded, and the creature on the work-table shrank, shrank, until a single dark orange kumquat stood in place of the impossible entity that had moments before occupied the spot.

"Voila," I said.

Victor composed himself, refastened his breeches, and leaned in to examine the kumquat on the table.

"Careful!" I cautioned him. "It's probably a perfectly ordinary kumquat, but one can't be entirely certain."

Victor prodded at it tentatively, then, when it failed to attack, he hefted it. "It was something quite extraordinary for a moment there."

"Indeed," I said. "The effects of ontological energies remain extremely unpredictable, and at first I had the very devil of a time fixing the more exotic alterations. Something about the masculine vital emanations is apparently unstable. But," I raised an eyebrow, "it turns out that with a suitable female to draw upon...."

Victor stared at me, his eyes widening. "Hargreaves wasn't lying!" he said at last.

I rolled my eyes in frustration. "I wasn't rogering his damned wife!" I said. "There is certainly an element of... indecorousness... to our researches, but the results speak for themselves."

"Results?"

"Three giant Pacific clams, three Argentine Lake Duck eggs, and, er, a lock of hair from my own head were on the table when the remarkably talented Mrs. Hargreaves attained her climax, and one outcome of the process was—"

"The Geoducks!" Victor exclaimed. Then his eyes sparkled with mischief. "I rather fancied I detected a familial resemblance there. But what feat of jesuitical pedantry was it when you denied rogering Mrs. Hargreaves, Daedalus?"

"You wound me, Victor. I am pledged to Knowledge as my only bride."

Victor drummed his fingers. "Hair-splitting does not become you."

I drew myself to my full height (my eyes still near half a foot below his, I confess). "I do not spend," I pronounced. "Thus, I conserve my Vital Fluids for intellectual pursuits, rather than carnal enjoyment. Celibacy is the Tesla family secret, passed down through the generations."

"Celibacy, passed down through the generations?" Victor asked dryly.

I flushed. "Its efficacy is not disproved by its imperfect application," I muttered.

There was a silence.

"So what do you propose?" Victor said at last.

Here the answer was clear enough. "We require a female," I said.

Victor shrugged. "Easily enough done," he said. "Shall I take the morning train down to London and return on the evening train with a suitable harlot?

"On the contrary," I answered him. "Such women, of necessity, have cultivated a degree of detachment from their labours that renders them distinctively unsuited to this task. Oh, what I wouldn't give for another Mrs. Hargreaves! She was a great asset to science. Her warm temperament, its ardour only sharpened by a decade of near-celibacy, her exceptional stamina, her magnificent posterior!"

Victor grinned. "Her posterior was an arse-et to science?"

My embarrassment to find that my recollections had momentarily gotten the better of me was considerable. "Her, er, stability upon the collecting platform was excellent. No danger of her falling off, none indeed."

"So how shall we procure another such?" Victor said, kindly changing the subject. "Perhaps we can make the rounds of the neighbouring estates: 'Pardon me, Madam, but do you find that your spending produces an ample quality of ectoplasmic emanation?'"

"No such inquiry should be necessary, fortunately. I have a cunning plan that should make discerning suitable subjects far simpler." I took a sheet of foolscap and began to sketch my design.

⤨

A couple of days later, the Erotometer was ready for testing. I pointed the collection trumpet at Victor. "Fix your mind upon a particularly pleasant lascivious recollection, if you would be so kind, old boy."

Victor gazed off into a far corner of the workshop, his eyes unfocused. "I happened to be in town yesterday, when Lady Wollaver arrived to pay the vicar a call. In stepping out of the carriage, she revealed almost her entire right calf, right there in the town square!"

The needle on the Erotometer jumped and held in a slightly elevated position. Success!

But before I could celebrate, the content of Victor's anecdote penetrated my preoccupied mind. "Blast! The vicar! He'll be visiting this afternoon! Damn country life and its infuriating distractions. No time to waste—we must get out of these grimy work clothes and prepare to receive visitors."

⤨

Reverend Pertwee, the vicar of —————shire, was a tallish, bent man, quite bald, with a long, ever-sniffling nose, thick spectacles of questionable efficaciousness, and a peculiar warble in his speech that I found quite distinctively irritating. With him on that day was a notably attractive young person who was unfamiliar to me.

"Mr. Tesla -sniff!" he addressed me when I stepped out to meet him. "What a pleasure it is to finally visit your charming grounds." He peered myopically about at the weed-choked garden, the unpruned orchard, the vine-covered walls. "Quite handsome -sniff. Yes, yes, quite -sniff handsome."

"I'm so glad you could make it, along with...?"

My prompt had the desired effect. "Oh! Oh! Yes, yes! -sniff Of course! Mr. Tesla, my daughter, Eleanor. Eleanor, this is Mr. Daedalus Tesla." She smiled and curtsied prettily. "Quite the richest man in three counties," the good reverend appended in a whisper so loud it fairly echoed from the manor walls. Eleanor sighed.

"Tesla," the vicar mused. "That's a foreign name, is it not? Hungarian, is it?"

"Serbian," I corrected him. "I'm afraid the —————shire Teslas are a scant three centuries in these parts, having constructed Tesla Hall in the reign of Queen Elizabeth. We are a restless people, and no doubt will be moving on again any century now."

Suddenly, Victor was at my side, a peculiar stunned expression on his visage.

"Reverend Pertwee, Miss Pertwee, allow me to present my assistant, Victor Dalrymple."

"A pleasure, Reverend," Victor murmured vaguely. Then he took one of Eleanor's hands in both of his own. "Good day, Miss Pertwee," he sighed. "I, er, I'm Victor Dalrymple."

"So I've heard," she answered sweetly, and, after a pause, extracted, with some small effort, her hand from his own.

I shall not recount the burdensome and tedious tea that followed. Suffice it to say that at the end of an hour-and-a-half, I knew more about the stomach ailments that the sheep of the local yeomen suffered from than I had expected to learn in my entire lifetime. Eventually, with some effort, I managed to insert a reference to the pressing business that called me and shoo him and his daughter, who had been largely silent, out the door.

I returned to my laboratory to find the Erotometer in ruins—its connectors scorched, the needle hopelessly bent, its glass shattered. My first impulse was to blame my pets, who milled anxiously at the other end of the room, but it soon became clear that it was not a fall or an impact that had done this damage. A quantity of Vital Fluid must have passed through the device too powerful for it to contain.

I shewed the ruins to Victor. "Is it just as you found it?" he asked.

I affirmed that it was.

"Then all we need do is trace the path of the collection trumpet, yes? Here... it points upwards, and towards the northwest corner of the room. So if nothing entered the laboratory in the interim, it would be picking up emanations from the sitting room, just by the fireplace."

"Absurd," I said. "No-one was in that side of the room but that milk-and-water daughter of the Vicar's. That meek little girl couldn't possibly have done that."

"On the contrary, Daedalus, I sensed from the moment I saw her that that girl has the most extraordinary depths."

I smiled. "What you sensed, my dear fellow, was a cockstand."

"Be that as it may, it looks like we may need to invite her back for further research."

I sighed resignedly. "If you can keep her unbearable father from coming along, I should be most grateful."

"I assure you that that is very much my intention."

Two days later, Victor notified me that Miss Pertwee would be visiting for a further tour of the grounds.

"Alone?" I asked, surprised at his resource.

"I assured the vicar that my patron, the esteemed and wealthy Daedalus Tesla, would be in attendance at all times."

With diligence, we completed several new, more robust Erotometers before the appointed time. We were upstairs in time to receive our guest, who, removed from her father's baleful penumbra, proved herself to be a reasonably charming young lady, bright and warm of manner, albeit with a sprinkling of freckles about her nose that bespoke an unseemly degree of exposure to sunlight.

After a short time, I excused myself, citing pressing work, and admonished the youths to be on their very best behavior.

In the laboratory, I removed the tele-phone from the hook, having previously taken like measure in the parlour. I pressed my ear to it just in time to hear Victor directing the girl to the seat she had occupied previously. The needle sprang to a position that, in Mrs. Hargreaves (for example), would have denoted the very acme of excitement.

From the earpiece I heard:

"I know that you are Mr. Tesla's assistant, but I do not quite grasp what you assist him at."

"Oh, business. Keeping the books, buying and selling, managing affairs, buying and selling, all that dreadful rubbish."

Eleanor nodded politely. "So then it was you who oversaw the purchase of those three massive steam engines last summer?"

"Oh, yes yes. That was I," he said quite truthfully. I winced, recognizing the trap the cunning little minx had laid. "Quite a lot of bother it was, too. Deuced things were unbelievably expensive."

"But what—?"

"UnbeLIEVably!"

"I'm sure. But what were they for?"

"For...? Oh, oh. Science. Scientific research. Thrilling, terribly modern stuff. Don't really understand it all that well myself. You'll have to ask old Daedalus to explain it to you some time."

The buck, as the Americans say, had been ably passed. It was not a conversation I looked forward to.

"Then he is really doing scientific research? Because..." she paused, and the needle on the Erotometer crept upward. "Rumor down in town has it that you two are up here rogering each other all the time."

A coughing fit from Victor followed. Apparently she had managed to time her remark to coincide with a mouthful of cake. When he got his breath back, he replied: "Oh, how perfectly ridiculous! I mean, we are, rather, from time to time. You know, when the mood strikes us. But not like that. I mean, I'm as fond of the ladies as the next fellow."

"Are you?" Eleanor said politely.

"Well, not to excess, of course," he appended, laughing nervously. "I mean, moderation in all things, what? I mean, I like some more than others, you know. I mean—dash it all, Miss Pertwee. I mean to say, I find you awfully charming." The needle responded to his confession with another modest gain. Miss Pertwee's output of Vital Fluids was now at approximately three times an ordinary Mathilde Hargreaves orgasm.

Eleanor laughed merrily. "You do have a certain fumbling charm yourself, Mr. Dalrymple," she conceded.

Soft sighs, and the gentle smacking sounds of tentative osculation followed, accompanied by a continued rise in the Erotometer's readings. The dial reached its maximum capacity, and I hastily unscrewed it and attached an even sturdier one I had prepared for such a contingency.

"Mr. Dalrymple," Miss Pertwee gasped after a time, "you take such liberties. Pray continue."

A bit later, Victor spoke: "Oh, Miss Pertwee, you are so lovely. May I call you Eleanor?"

"You may, dear Victor. Tell me: have you copulated with a great many women?"

"Oh, er, I say. That's a rather personal question, isn't it?"

"Yes."

There was a silence.

"Several," he ventured at last.

"That is more than adequate. Might I induce you to initiate me into these mysteries?"

"To... to..."

"Take me, yes."

"Miss Pertwee, wherever did you get such ideas?"

"French novels, of course. I had a school friend with a remarkably extensive collection. And I believe you have permission to address me as Eleanor."

"French novels. Of course," Victor echoed. The needle on the Erotometer was starting to flag a bit.

"I, er... I would be delighted to assist you in such an endeavour," he ventured. "Really, extremely delighted."

"Marvelous," said Eleanor. "The moment I saw you, I thought you might be just the man to instruct me in these matters. I am certain you are not one of those dreary fellows one reads of who demand that their lady friends be in possession of a maidenhead. Mine was taken by a marrow two years ago."

"A marrow, Miss Pertwee? The vegetable? That the Italians call *il zucchine?*"

"The very same. A most particularly bold and impetuous hot-house marrow. It was quite the ravishment, I can assure you."

"I consider it no dishonor at all to be preceded by so noble an agricultural product. But... er... this is most probably neither the place nor the time. Servants will still be about. Perhaps we can meet at a later hour...?"

"Are you certain? I think if you were to pursue the matter now, you might find me quite... receptive."

There was a rustling sound. The meter jumped, but it was Victor who gasped. "Oh lord," he breathed, barely audible through the speaker, "how hot your cunny is."

"Are you certain we haven't time for a brief lesson today? Oh! That does feel quite lovely. I shall—ohhh—still require—aaaah—more extensive training at a—oh my!—later date."

"Well, I suppose a—a brief lesson is unlikely to do any harm. Let us see... could you recline here over this ottoman?"

The Erotometer flagged as Miss Pertwee moved from the centre of the collection field to its perimeter.

"Now let me just raise up these skirts...."Victor said. "What a beautiful bottom you have!"

The needle began to rise again.

"Oh, my," came Eleanor's voice. "What is that lovely smell?"

"Smell? I'm afraid I don't..."

The needle's rise, rather than leveling off, was increasing in rapidity.

"Victor, dear. I find myself quite urgently in need. Pray, pray, do not make me wait."

"Certainly not, my precious dove. Here, do you feel me at your—"

He was interrupted by a piercing shriek from Eleanor. I attempted to adjust the angle of the Erotometer collection trumpet and recoiled, singed by the heat radiating from the device.

"Hush, hush," he urged her anxiously. "There are others about."

Her joyous shrieks subsided somewhat, but did not cease.

"Harder" she called out. "Fuck me—harummmff!" Clearly Victor had clamped a hand over her mouth, effectively muffling her screams of delight. My eyes were fixed to the tele-phone in amazement, which proved fortunate a moment later when the Erotometer's dial exploded, showering the back of my head with shards of glass, and producing a sudden silence above.

"What was that?" said Victor.

"It sounded terribly close by," Eleanor said breathlessly.

The muffled sounds of hasty rearrangement ensued, followed by a leave-taking characterized by discomfort and ardour. Anxious to resume their lesson, they arranged to meet for supper in his apartments the very next day. She promised that she would find some way to mollify her father on this point; he promised her an abundance of privacy, and with numerous protestations of eagerness for the following evening, they parted.

❧

Scant moments later, I was at the sink, carefully picking shards of glass out of my hair, when the door to the laboratory swung open, and Victor bounded down the steps. "I must have her!" the two of us said at the same moment.

"I say!" Victor declared. "I won't have you experimenting upon Eleanor like some... crabapple! She is far too delicate and precious a creature for that!"

"And you are far too malleable and sentimental a creature for Science," I retorted. "But have no fear, my friend. I have no interest in experimenting upon her. No, I want her as a source of motive force. I needn't lay hands upon her at all, if it offends your delicate sensibilities so very much."

"Is this another of your jesuitical sophistries, Tesla? If you don't intend to touch her, how to you purpose to extract her Vital Fluids?"

"My dear fellow, she is obviously besotted with you," I said smoothly. "I am certain that if you were to induce her to come down here for you to make love to her, she would positively jump at the notion."

"I suppose…. Besotted, you say? You really think so?"

And a moment later: "Great Scott! What happened to our lovely Erotometer?"

I smiled. "Your delicate and precious creature blasted it to Hades with the force of her lust. I say… which ottoman was it that you bent her over?"

"The black leather one. Why, are you concerned about its hygiene?"

"Simply curious," I said, but my mind was working furiously. The girl had spoken of a marvelous smell, which Victor was entirely unable to detect, just after reclining upon the ottoman and just before her paroxysms of desire became so destructively intense. That ottoman was the favoured resting place of my pets on idle week-end mornings when I was taking in the Sunday Times. It seemed to me entirely possible that the hour of the Geoducks had come at last.

Several days later, Victor and Eleanor met once more. They dined, they retired to his chambers, and he initiated her more fully into the arts of love; they attained the very acme of enjoyment in each other's arms, achieving divine bliss such as few mortals have known, &c. &c. My own attention was elsewhere, as I attempted to modernize and refine the Ontological Engine to accommodate quantities of Vital Fluids that had been hitherto inaccessible. But from my assistant's interminable prattle about it the next day, one would think he had singlehandedly invented sexual intercourse.

"Daedalus," he said to me, "I am in love."

"You are certainly in an elevated state of chemical excitation," I replied. "Do you suppose that your paramour is nearly ready to participate in our project?"

Victor scratched his chin speculatively. "She may very well be," he mused. "She wishes to enact 'The Naughty Schoolgirl and the Strict Headmaster' on Thursday and 'The Abduction of the Sabine Women' on Friday. Perhaps I can propose 'The Mad Doctor and His Crabapple' for Saturday."

"If your strength keeps up," I said. "Wherever did she—?"

"French novels, apparently."

Some days later, over breakfast, Victor announced, "Oh, by the way: Eleanor has said that she wishes to better make your acquaintance."

"Whatever for?" I asked.

"I believe she wishes to thank you for your distinctively laissez-faire approach to chaperonage."

"Well, doesn't that rather defeat the purpose? I mean, if my most charming quality is my absence, it seems like paying a call on me can only serve to mitigate it."

"Shall I tell her that you have declined her offer, then?"

"Oh, not at all. I should be delighted to dine with her. You will be joining us, of course?"

"Of course."

On the appointed date, however, Victor received a telegram from London. "D--n! Blast! Bugger!" he shouted at it, an expostulation which apparently failed to alter the text in any wise, though the messenger boy who had delivered it did blush.

"I must go to London at once," he announced. "The Daguerreotype Society is receiving its new photo-graphic machine, and if Prichard gets his hands on it, I'll never see the damned thing."

"A brother in your Society is known to be larcenous?"

"Clumsy. He's shattered three cameras beyond repair already this year."

I nodded. "I'll give Miss Pertwee your regrets, then."

Victor looked suspiciously at me. "You will not touch her."

"I am pledged to Knowledge—"

"—as your only bride. Yes, yes. Matrimony is not the prospect that concerns me here. Give me your word, Daedalus."

"You have my word as a gentleman and a scientist, Victor. I shall not lay hands on Miss Pertwee."

"Very well, then. Will you have your driver take me to the rail station in a half-hour?"

As Victor prepared to go, my mind was furiously at work. I would honour my pledge to him, of course. But if my speculations as to the ultimate qualities of the Geoducks was true, my own hands need not be the instrument of Miss Pertwee's ravishment. Victor might be a bit disconcerted at first by my plans, but once he grasped the immeasurable boon to science, I was sure any reservations would be cast aside. Barely had the clattering of hooves announced Victor's departure than I began my preparations.

Dinner was a pleasant affair. Miss Pertwee was a lively companion, with an ample supply of light conversation, and a surprisingly sound grasp, for a female, of the sciences. She displayed a great interest in my tales of clever young cousins Ralph and Nikola, recent emigrants from the Old Country to America, and pressed me for what details of life there could be gleaned from their infrequent letters.

In the sitting room afterward, she acquired a somewhat more serious demeanor. "Mr. Tesla. As I believe you know, your assistant and I have become quite fond of each other. However, he remains quite perplexingly oblique about the work that you do here."

The prospect of explaining my researches, a notion which had hitherto filled me with apprehension, now seemed extremely fortuitous as a means for introducing her to her proposed role in my schemes.

"Are you familiar with the term 'ontology,' Miss Pertwee?"

"It is a concept from theology, is it not? The categories to which things can be assigned."

"Your understanding of its conventional meaning is fair enough, but its use is no longer confined to the dusty tomes of theologians. I myself have made several novel discoveries with regard to the art of manipulating these categories scientifically."

"Manipulating the categories? I'm not at all sure I grasp your meaning. Do you mean using one word to name a thing, rather than another? That hardly sounds like the work of scientists."

"Oh, no," I laughed. "Not the names of the thing, but the actual thing itself. You see, the categories in which we place things are far more malleable than we perceive. Our presumption that a thing is itself and no other is essentially a convenient fiction. Take, er—" I cast about for a suitably neutral example, and my eyes fell upon the telephone. "—this tele-phone here. How can we assert with confidence that it is a tele-phone and not, say, a camera?"

Eleanor looked at me with a combination of three parts perplexity and one part mirth.

"Why, because it does not take photographs," she said in the patient tones with which one addresses a nursery child.

I waved this objection aside. "But what if it were to take pictures, what would it be then?"

"A tele-phone... that takes pictures?" She burst into silvery peals of laughter. "Oh, Mr. Tesla, how funny you are!"

With a visible effort, she composed herself, blinking rapidly with her hands folded demurely in her lap. Then she happened to glance once more at the tele-phone, and all was lost. She rolled about on the divan in paroxysms of unrestrained mirth that bordered, to be quite frank, on the unladylike. "You could call it a camera-phone," she fairly shrieked, tears rolling down her face as she howled in delight at her own jape.

Well, this was a bit thick. I'd rather softened towards the girl up to this point, but now I was taking a certain unsavoury pleasure in the prospect of teaching this frivolous creature to respect the power of my Ontological Engine.

"Giggle all you wish, Miss Pertwee," I said, grinding my teeth together. She looked at me quizzically, quietly wiping the tears from her flushed cheeks. "But know that the manipulation of ontological fields is no mere theory. Rather, I have succeeded in harnessing these forces with an engine of my own devising, and have thus twisted the very nature of reality to my own ends."

Thereat, I tugged at a cord that pulled the curtain away from the box that housed my pets. Awakened by the sudden light, they raised their siphons and cast them tentatively about, shaking their wings in a desultory fashion.

"Oh!" Eleanor cried, standing and clasping her hands to her mouth as the creatures rose and began to waddle purposefully towards her. I smiled in grim satisfaction.

"The dear little creatures! Have they names?" she said.

In retrospect, it is clear that I should have realized that their haberdashery did not present the 'ducks in their most formidable aspect. The purposed ravishment appeared, for the time being, well derailed.

Chagrined, I had little choice but to make the introductions. "The largest, in the derby hat, is Hubert." Hubert bowed, and Eleanor squealed in delight.

"The one in the bonnet is Louise." She, too, inclined her siphon.

"And the smallest, with the drop of fluid at the lip of his siphon, is Dewey, the brightest and most sensitive of the lot." Dewey, for his part, jumped up and down excitedly, and scrambled up onto his favourite ottoman.

"Oh, you dear thing!" Eleanor said. "I shall give you a kiss."

She leaned down to press her lips to Dewey's wrinkled siphon. He angled it upward to approach her. As she came within a couple inches of him, her nostrils flared, and a flushed suffused her face. A rattling behind me unmistakably bespoke the profound agitation of the Erotometer I had arrayed for such a circumstance.

"Oh, my," Eleanor breathed. "What was I—?"

"You were going to give Dewey a kiss," I reminded her gently.

"Oh yes! Of course." Her lips brushed his moist siphon tip; girl and Geoduck each froze in place, trembling. Her cheeks had taken on a great deal of colour now; her mouth slowly opened, and she took the full head of his siphon into her mouth, breathing heavily through her nose.

"Miss Pertwee," I said. She yelped in surprise, and Dewey quacked and flapped his wings as the momentary spell was broken. A glance over my shoulder shewed that the needle on the Erotometer was dropping rapidly as she attempted to compose herself.

"You... you made these creatures yourself?" she asked, anxious, I think, to resume more normal discourse.

"The privilege of creation is one that belongs only to God," I said with laudable humility. "Say rather that I... assembled them, according to certain purposes of my own. Would you care to see the equipment I use for such work?"

"Certainly, certainly. Lead on, Mr. Tesla, and I shall follow."

I led Miss Pertwee down the creaking staircase to my laboratory, the three Geoducks following after her in a neat little line. I pointed out the categorical condensers and the energetic accumulator, and I gave her a brief precis of the functioning of the vitality stabilization array.

She seemed yet flushed and a bit abstracted, but she strove mightily to attend to my words. "This is what those steam engines were purchased to power, then?"

"Indeed. There they sit now," I said, gesturing to the sooty tanks, their mighty pistons gathering dust.

"...But they don't seem to be attached to the other equipment..."

"Very astute! I believe I have discovered a superior power source. This equipment here should allow me to harness far greater forces than I have hitherto been able to access. Would you care for a demonstration?"

The Geoducks were milling about our feet, rubbing their siphons against our limbs, apparently sensing, somehow, the events to come. "If it will help me to understand Victor's perplexing secretiveness, I would be most grateful for one," Miss Pertwee said.

"I promise that you will find it most illuminating," I told her, and held out my arm to Dewey. He spread his wings and, flapping them frantically, rose slowly into the air before settling upon my forearm.

"Hold him for me, would you, my dear?" I said, thrusting the Geoduck into her arms, where he immediately began to nuzzle affectionately at her.

"Excellent. Now if you'll just don this circlet here..." I carefully placed the metal ring upon her head. A deep hum arose immediately from the engine, as her prodigious reserves of Vital Fluids began to animate the machinery.

"I... I feel rather faint," she said.

"Here, why don't you sit down." I directed her to the padded bench behind her. Hubert deftly lifted her skirts with his siphon. In a moment he had disappeared from view, his derby rolling away into a corner.

"Oh! Mr. Tesla! Your... your pet!"

"I do believe they like you, Miss Pertwee. That's a very good sign—they are excellent judges of character."

"Can not you retrieve him? He's being—aiee!—being rather rude, I fear." Her hands were still occupied cradling Dewey, who nuzzled most warmly at her cheeks. She shifted about in a most agitated fashion, but her legs remained parted.

I shook my head sadly. "I am afraid not. I made a solemn promise to Victor not to touch you."

"But he is—ummf!" Whatever liberties Hubert was taking with her lower parts went unreported as Dewey's siphon found her parted lips and slid within.

Beside us, the humming rose in volume and pitch. Eleanor's muffled cries gave way to moaning as she suckled at Dewey's formidable siphon, drawing forth more fluid of love, which she swallowed with apparent relish.

She reclined further and released Dewey, who now stood upon her heaving bosom, thrusting his siphon slowly between the young lady's inviting lips and gurgling with delight. Her feet left the ground and her skirts fell about her waist, revealing a tableau of unforgettable lasciviousness. Her stockings ended just above her well-shaped calves; bare creamy thighs then rose, joining at a plump and well-furred motte that failed utterly to cover the prominent labia minora that glistened seductively beneath. Hubert nuzzled eagerly at that apex, apparently uncertain how to proceed with his object of desire.

Never fear, Hubert. Abler hands are prepared to assist you.

Blindly, Eleanor groped beneath her waist, until one delicate hand closed upon his siphon. He squawked at the force of her grip, but then his sighs of pleasure joined her own groans as she rubbed his tip along her opening. Geoduck and human anticipatory fluid commingled, forming strands that connected their dueling organs of pleasure. Hubert clambered onto the bench, his new position affording him vastly superior purchase. Then, with a tug of Eleanor's wrist, he was within her. Her stifled rhythmic cries drew my attention to her mouth once more, where Dewey, astoundingly, was buried nearly to his shoulders, flapping his wings wildly for balance as he thrust into her throat.

As I watched, he shuddered and twitched, feathers flying through the close air of the laboratory. Eleanor gulped and sputtered as he spent deep within her throat. Then, inch by inch by inch, Dewey's sated siphon withdrew until only the tip was brushing Eleanor's lips. Tenderly he kissed her lips, her cheeks, her forehead, before rolling over onto his back beside her head, as limp as a corpse.

In that moment's respite I realized: these fascinating proceedings, revealing as they did facets of the character of my pets on which I had previously only been able to speculate, had for a time blinded me to my primary work. The Ontological Engine stood, humming and crackling with the vast forces flowing into it, and I had neglected to place anything upon the work-table for it to alter!

Frantically, I looked about the laboratory for some suitable object. Thus far, I had been able permanently to affect only living things, or parts freshly plucked from some living creature. It was entirely possible that, with the energies available to me now, that barrier would crumble. On the other hand, what a tragedy it would be if some inert object rendered the entire ambitious experiment useless! My eyes fell upon Dewey, still prone upon the Collection Stand, gurgling and twitching happily. Could a product of previous ontological manipulation be altered once more? Certainly it was an intriguing question, ripe to be tested.

It was the work of a moment to spring to the Collection Stand and gently lift Dewey from it. At first, he cooed and nuzzled against me, but as I approached the very work-table where I had created him, he grew agitated, spreading his wings and kicking at me with his webbed feet as I attempted to place him where the beams would shortly be falling. I seized a disused birdcage from a corner of the room and hastily thrust the now-frantic creature within, shutting the door behind him. Hastily I positioned the rocking, loudly-protesting package upon the table and dashed to the controls.

I returned my attention to the Collection Stand and found that Eleanor was well advanced in the throes of pleasure, her brow knit, her face darkly flushed as she neared what promised to be the first climax of many. Every minute or two Hubert would withdraw the shining, wrinkled length of his siphon to draw a quick gasping breath, Eleanor's well-used nether parts receiving no time to recover from his formidable girth before being distended once more.

There was no time to waste. I activated the Engine, and the blue glow came rushing out of the collectors in a veritable torrent, suffusing the work-table with a near-blinding radiance. At once, foot-tall vortices of light eddied away, illuminating every corner of my basement laboratory, until they burst with audible cracks upon the damp stone walls. Nearby, Eleanor's legs kicked in the air as her hands scrabbled for purchase at the sides of the bench and she screamed at the apex of her enjoyment.

Hubert, it seems, was a more considerate lover than I might have given him credit for. He paused in his thrusting to accommodate his partner's aftermath, grinding his shoulders in slow circles against Eleanor's swollen mound. As she panted, the radiance continued flowing from the Ontological Engine onto the still-rocking cage on the work-table, the metal of the cage sending forth an answering glow that obscured whatever was transpiring within. One of the vortices of ontological force that broke loose from the Engine brushed Hubert, his gleaming siphon still resting within Eleanor's interior, and a single magnificent pea-cock feather sprouted from his posterior.

In this interval of relative calm, her eyes met mine. "Oh, Mr. Tesla! Your pets are a marvel! But tell me, I pray—might they do me an injury?"

"An injury?" I inquired.

"If they spend inside me... is there any chance of... harm?"

"Oh! You are afraid of them impregnating you. Rest assured, my dear, your ova and Geoduck spermatozoa are entirely incompatible."

"Oh, thank you, Mr. Tesla. That is a great comfort to me. But... wouldn't you like to join in our festivities here? I'm sure you have a very handsome prick, and—" here she looked down at the front of my trousers "—I can see that it must be giving you terrible discomfort."

"You are very kind, Miss Pertwee, but I am pledged to Knowledge as my only bride."

But no answer was forthcoming, for Hubert had resumed his vigourous thrusts, and she was entirely preoccupied with the sensations she was experiencing.

This time, Hubert was able to join Eleanor, his webbed feet scrabbling at her milky thighs, leaving faint crisscrossed pink welts across them as he shuddered within her. Eleanor bit down upon the knuckles of one hand, the other cradling Hubert's shell between her lofted legs. The surge in ontological energies produced created another crop of crackling vortices. I saw one strike the collection stand, where a tiny palm tree sprouted from the wood, laden with gooseberry-sized cocoanuts.

When their mutual climax had subsided, Hubert crawled up Eleanor's panting body to lie, similarly spent, where his brother had rested, his one over-sized tail-feather extending past Eleanor's knees.

"My goodness," Eleanor said when she could again speak. "That was quite extraordinary." The radiance from the Engine began to subside, the unearthly hum to soften. I clenched my fists in frustration. Too soon! I was certain that this woman could give forth more Vital Fluids, if only my agents were equal to the task. A moment later, there was a great fluttering of wings, and Louise settled herself between Eleanor's yet-widespread thighs.

"It would appear that your ordeal may not yet be over." I said, relieved. "Louise would seem to be manifesting some Sapphic tendencies." Now, indeed, it was her turn to snuffle about Eleanor's red and dilated orifice, running as it was with her brother's spend, which she proceeded to slurp up with all apparent relish, while Eleanor began once again to moan at the pleasant friction thus produced.

"Oh, dear, dear Louise," she moaned, "do please fuck me. I find myself still very much in need." Eagerly Louise complied, pressing the tip of her siphon to Eleanor's opening and working it, by steady increments, inside. As I stood watching this coupling, a most perverse idea came to me, which stood an excellent chance of increasing the girl's Vital Fluid output still further, if such a thing was possible. I left the control panel for a moment and made certain preparations for my scheme. Then I crouched by the recumbent young lady and spoke thus into her ear:

"By the way, Eleanor, do you happen to know anything about bivalve reproduction?"

Unable to gather breath or thought sufficient for speech now that the erotic frenzy was once more upon her, she shook her head mutely.

"It's really quite an interesting subject," I said. "You see, as you've had occasion to note, most male siphon-clams spurt their seed forth from their siphons, leaving their sperm to adventure, willy-nilly through the seas, in quest of their female counterparts. That much is unsurprising.

"What you may find more noteworthy is that the females, by and large, expend their fluid of generation in precisely the same manner." Her eyes came unfocused. I was losing her attention—I had to get to the point.

"That is to say, the female expends her ova through her siphon as well, in the hopes that the sperm and eggs may come together in a suitably congenial environment for them to grow."

Her brow was furrowing further—she was beginning to suspect my meaning. "...and I very much fear," I continued, "that your tender young womb may prove to be just such an environment." Behind me, the pitch of the Ontological Engine rose to a frightening whine. The radiance cast was as stark as at the moment of a lightning-strike. The little strumpet was excited by the idea!

Her eyes, however, widened in dismay. "Oh lord! What shall I do, Mr. Tesla?"

"Well, you could always try asking Louise to stop."

She gathered her breath. "Louise! Louise, darling, I... I..." She sobbed in frustration. "Oh, it feels so exquisitely lovely, I somehow can't bear to have her stop, howsoever much I might wish it!"

I nodded sympathetically. "If you could induce her to spend elsewhere, I should think there would be no danger in that. But of course, it would have to be somewhere where neither of her brothers had ejaculated."

She blinked at me in perplexity.

"Try inviting her to penetrate your bottom."

She gaped in astonishment. "That's impossible!" she exclaimed.

"Not at all. In fact, I think you will find that it can be a source of quite remarkable pleasure. Here, raise your legs a bit further, and I will give you a taste of the joys to be thus gained."

Obediently, she brought her limbs up, hooking her arms under her knees and thus exposing the exquisitely pretty little pink knot between the cheeks of her bottom.

Already I had in my hand a slender metal dildoe, anointed with pomade. I wriggled it against her bottom-hole for a moment, allowing her to accustom herself to the sensation. Oh, her howls when I slowly pressed the object into her! Were they of delight or dismay? I was beyond certainty, beyond caring. The whine behind me rose in pitch once more, now accompanied by a rattling noise unmistakable even through the rest of the din.

"Say it, Eleanor," I demanded, my hand working the dildoe steadily into her. "Tell Louise what you desire."

"Oh!" she cried out. "Take my bottom-hole, Louise!"

There was a moment's hesitation, then Louise extracted her siphon from Eleanor's slick cunny and cocked it as if listening.

"Go on," I urged her.

"I want to feel your great affair spend in my bottom, Louise!" Eleanor cried, squirming her hips in a way that lent powerful credence to her words. "Please, bugger my arse-hole!"

By this time the dildoe had vacated Eleanor's rear passage. Louise wasted no time in pressing her siphon against Eleanor's tiny orifice, pressing within with a patience and consideration that appeared only to inflame Eleanor, who rocked her hips impatiently against the massive tool, her fingers working frantically on her inflamed clitoris.

In time, the defenses of Eleanor's sphincter were breached, and the great blunt head of Louise's siphon passed within, accompanied by a veritable symphony of shrieking from Eleanor.

I stood by the side of the bench, surveying this thrilling tableau.

"More," Eleanor was moaning deliriously. "Need more..."

One of her flailing hands struck the front of my breeches and grasped my rigid member with spasmodic force. With the strength of one possessed, she tore my breeches open. "Miss Pertwee!" I started to object, but already she had risen on her elbows and taken my cock into her hot mouth.

Vaguely I remembered the words of my oath to Victor, and clenched my hands at my sides, refusing to lay hands on my ravisher.

She drew back to look at me with great beseeching eyes, my cock still firmly gripped in her hand. "Please, Mr. Tesla, I beg of you—fuck me? I long to have this handsome great prick in my poor hungry cunny—I think I shall die without it!"

Well, I reasoned, a momentary penetration could do no harm, so long as I avoided ejaculation. Hastily, I pulled off my boots and breeches and straddled Louise, who was by this point working furiously in Eleanor's bottom.

The liquid heat and compression of Eleanor's cunt was exquisite. I almost lost control of myself at that moment, but decades of stern self-discipline asserted themselves, and I held myself still until the fit had passed. Then, just as self-restraint had begun to assert itself, the vixen locked her legs about my waist and began to undulate in a most stimulating manner.

"Miss Pertwee, I shall spend!" I cried in dismay.

"Yes, yes!" she answered "Spend in me, both of you!" I heard a terrible crackling behind me, but I was powerless in Eleanor's grip and in the rush of emotions and sensations that overwhelmed me. A wash of sensation such as I have never known came over me, shaking my brains in my head like dice in a cup as I shuddered and pounded atop Eleanor's spread legs. Eleanor's shrieks crescendoed once more, her nails digging painfully into my bottom. I heard a great tumultuous noise, as of a mighty cataract roaring off a cliff. I opened my eyes just in time to see a huge vortex of ontological energies, quite four feet in height, hurling towards me. There was a massive roar, an intolerably bright blue glow, and a rush of heat.

I awoke on the laboratory floor and attempted to stagger to my feet, but found my perspective oddly skewed, as if the entire room had vastly increased in size. My Ontological Engine was in shambles, pieces scattered about the laboratory. The cage, thrown from the upended work-table, was burst asunder, an iron blossom whose skeletal blackened petals reached outward in every direction.

Miss Pertwee lay upon her back on the Collection Stand, a beatific smile upon her face, her skirts still bunched chaotically about her waist. The stand itself was a riot of blossoms of all manner of shapes, sizes, and colours.

Over me now crouched an unfamiliar youth, entirely nude, slender and angelic of aspect, gold ringlets falling about a gentle face that was contorted into a look of deep concern. "Uncle," said the boy, "is that you?"

"Young man, I do not believe I have your acquaintance," I said. Or intended to, but only an inchoate gurgling reached my ears.

"Uncle Daedalus?" he persisted. "It is I, Dewey! I was so terribly afraid, but I should have known that you would only have my best interests at heart! This is a wonderful gift you have given me!"

A terrible suspicion rose in me. I raised my hands to my face, or so I intended. Instead two feathered wings met my horrified gaze.

I recall little of the subsequent hours. When Victor returned from London the following morning, I suspect that Eleanor's precis of the night's events may have omitted certain unnecessary details of what had transpired. I likewise suspect that what narrative she did not provide, conjecture filled in amply enough. That afternoon there was a council of war. Eleanor, Victor, Dewey (now garbed in my own clothes, which fit him well enough), Hubert, Louise, and myself all met in my study to devise a course of action.

"Daedalus," said Victor, "I am not well pleased. I suspect that you did not honour the spirit of your pledge to me, and I am certain that you took reckless and imprudent risks with more than one innocent soul entrusted into your care."

Well, this was a fine situation! There my so-called protégé, who had abandoned me when I needed him most, stood, with all his parts and functions intact, scolding me—I, who had lost all in selfless pursuit of Science. I let him know, in no uncertain terms, of my own assessment of his loyalty, his competence, his moral fibre, his intellect, and his likely ancestry. It was only after several minutes of this forceful rebuke that I calmed down enough to realize that only squawks and gurgles were emerging as I flapped my wings furiously, and I lapsed into mortified silence.

Dewey cleared his throat. "Uncle Daedalus says that he is very sorry for the hurt that his reckless actions have caused, and is very eager to make amends in whatever ways remain in his power. He adds that his sole intent was to allow me to walk among you in the form you see now and that he hopes that the nobility of his goals can, in some small way, mitigate the imprudence of his methods." He looked at me with an utterly unreadable expression. "Isn't that right, Uncle?"

There was a moment's hesitation. Then I nodded.

∾

Little remains to be told. Two days of penmanship practice sufficed to allow me to take pen in siphon and produce a document leaving, in the event of my unexpected disappearance, my estate in the trusteeship of Mr. Dalrymple, pending my eventual return.

Victor has turned his hand to rebuilding the Ontological Engine, though work proceeds slowly due to my limited capacity for mechanical labor. However, my improved design should guard in the future against such a transfer of ontological status from one subject to another as happened that fateful night. Dewey shows significant potential in his grasp of ontological theory and is already an asset in the laboratory—I confess myself quite proud of him.

Victor and Eleanor are engaged to be married. Signs of a possible pending blessed event make an imminent ceremony desirable. After some weeks of quiet discussion, Victor and Eleanor decided to invite Dewey, Hubert, and Louise to join them in Victor's apartments, where the shouts and quacks of delight often extend until the cock's crow. A like offer was extended to myself, but I was of course was forced to decline. Despite the monstrous pressures this form exerts upon my libido, the experiences of that night have served only to remind me of the necessity of celibacy for the truly first-rate scientific mind, and the dire consequences of any lapse.

Miss Pierce's Position

At some unknown hour during a more-than-ordinarily damp and blustery October night at Tesla Hall, I became a man.

At daybreak I half-awoke, naked and shivering, with the vague, uneasy awareness that something of great significance had occurred, though whether for the better or worse I could not yet limn. I gathered my bedclothes about me, pulling the coverlet over my head to shield my eyes from the early light. Then I froze, heightened wakefulness bringing with it awareness of my altered physique.

With a joyous yell, I sprang from the bed to pose before my dressing-mirror. The unutterably welcome sight that greeted my eyes was of an exceptionally well-formed man of early middle years, dark-complected, of no great stature, with the characteristic high forehead and long fingers of one intended by Nature for greatness in the sciences. "Hum-hum," I said experimentally, flexing my fingers. A faint hoarseness appeared to be the only residue of my prior ordeal. "Tra-la-la," I ventured. "The rain in Spain falls, despite popular misapprehension, almost entirely in the hills." My visage, my voice, my hands were all restored to me.

Heedless of my nudity, I bounded into the corridor, calling out, "Victor, Eleanor, Dewey! Come look! Come look!" I flung open the door of every room I passed, but found none to witness my delight. Then I recalled that the newlyweds were in London for the weekend, traveling with Eleanor's father, the reverend Theophilus Pertwee, a fate I would not wish on my most hated foe.

My "nephew" Dewey—our consanguinity both greater and less than is properly contained in that word—was then to be the sole human witness of my startling transformation. I dashed to his door and paused for a moment. Sounds of motion came from within; good! He, too, had arisen early, and would be in fit state to appreciate my transformation.

I opened the door and beheld—not the fair youth who had resided in the room lo these last several months, but an entirely different creature framed in the doorway, largely anatine in profile, with the webbed feet and feathered wings and tail of an Argentine lake duck. It displayed unmistakable ostraceous qualities as well, to wit the calciferous shell that enclosed its body, and the wrinkled, naked, disconcertingly phallic siphon that stood it in stead of a head and neck, seeing and hearing quite adequately despite the lack of any visible sensory organs. In short, it was unmistakably one of the duck/clam hybrids which my mastery of ontological engineering had brought into being some years before.

"Louise!" I said to it. "Where is your——?" But wait. The plumage of the creature before me was unmistakably male. "Hubert, rather. How did——?" But the Geoduck I beheld was too small and slight of built to be Hubert. It was only then that I observed the telltale bead of fluid that quivered at the tip of its siphon. "Dewey," I breathed wonderingly.

Dewey—for it was indeed he—quacked and gurgled merrily, bouncing and flapping his wings.

"The ontological fields must have faded at last!" I mused aloud.

Months had passed since the dreadful accident that had left my laboratory in ruins and myself imprisoned in a grotesque form like the one that now stood before me. Months of humiliation, isolation, and painfully slow scientific research. Months, also, tormented by the volcanic amorousness of the preternaturally libidinous Geoduck; passions I was forced to suppress, celibacy being of course the fundamental necessity of any productive intellectual labour.

The one bright spot in that disastrous event had been that one of the three Geoduck creatures of my own creation had been elevated to humanity just as I had been debased. A lesser man might have begrudged him that, but remembering the old adage, *The finder's goods shall he retain / Nor mind the loser's dreadful pain,* I rejoiced, rather, in his good fortune.

Likewise, my new elation was now tempered by compassion—an emotion to which I have always been exceptionally vulnerable—as I contemplated Dewey's fate. He had been vouchsafed a fleeting membership in the glorious race of Man, the very crown of creation, and now he was relegated to walk upon the earth a mere beast once more.

"But you, my dear nephew! We must find a way to restore your humanity. We shall find a way!"

I dressed hurriedly and let myself into the basement laboratory, where I surveyed my bent and blackened Ontological Engine. Four months of work by Victor and Dewey, overseen—as much as possible—by my transformed self, had barely begun the work of undoing what one disastrous night had wrought.

But now my own hands were turned to the task, and matters would proceed with greater haste. I donned a well-worn work apron, took tools in hand, and set to work.

The thick windows flush with the ceiling of my laboratory were letting in a little late-morning sun and I was whistling merrily between my teeth when a discreet knock at the basement door announced my butler. When I answered the door, he twitched a bit in startlement, but rapidly recovered himself.

"Master Tesla, you have returned," he said.

"Obviously, Wilson."

"Welcome back, sir."

Such long-winded sentimentalism sets my teeth on edge, and I attempt to discourage it in my servants. "You had something to say to me."

"Oh, yes, sir. Or rather, I expected to find Master Dalrymple in the laboratory with one of those... creatures. But now that you are returned, you are most probably the superior choice for the matter at hand."

There was a pause. "Which is...?" I prompted him impatiently.

"There is a person at the door who insists on speaking to the master of the house. "He furrowed his brow. "Something about being an engineer in need of a position, sir."

"Well!" I said, brightening. "If the fellow is any good at all, that shows excellent timing and admirable initiative."

"Oh, no, sir. It isn't—"

"None of your fussing, Wilson. Lead me to him at once."

But when we reached the sitting-room, there was none there but a plump little woman—if you might call her that—in an outlandish bicycle-suit featuring a pair of broad trousers in the Bloomer style. Her medium-brown hair was in appalling disarray, her skin flushed as if from exertion or high emotion. She stood as I entered and strode towards me. "Mr. Dalrymple, I presume?" she said, meeting my eye in an entirely unladylike manner.

"You do indeed," I answered crisply, "and no."

I paused for her apology. When none appeared to be forthcoming, I resumed. "I am Daedalus Tesla, of Tesla Hall. You are associated in some capacity with the engineer I was invited to meet?"

She grinned an overconfident, ironical sort of grin. "Mr. Tesla! I had heard you were on an extended vacation, so I did not anticipate the honour of your acquaintance. I am Minerva Pierce, of no particular place, and I am the engineer in question."

I laughed politely at this jest. "A lady engineer?" My tone, I think, made clear that, of the sentence's three words, two were used with some reservation.

"If you like. Word has reached me of some rather exciting developments in ontological science in these latitudes, and I am here to offer my services."

"You are here to offer your services," I echoed incredulously. "Well, we have no need of the services of a lady engineer at this time, amusing though the concept might be. If we find ourselves in want of such a creature in the future, rest assured that we shall contact you at once. Good morning."

"Sir," she persisted. "You doubt my competence due to my sex. But I am not merely skilled with tools, but well-versed in ontological theory as well. Put any test to me and I shall show you my merit!"

At this point I had really had quite enough of this impertinent woman. "Oh, you've shown me your merit quite enough already," I told her. "Barging into my home in a ludicrous harem suit, hectoring my domestic staff, and pretending to knowledge of matters entirely beyond your comprehension. Now, you must excuse me, I have business of some importance to attend to."

I turned to my butler. "Wilson, if Miss... er... Pierce has any difficulty seeing herself out, please assist her in her prompt exit."

Mood now thoroughly ruined, I headed back towards my laboratory to try to salvage some utility from my day.

Dewey, it transpired, had crept to the top of the basement stairs to catch a glimpse of our visitor. *Who?* he quacked as I began my descent.

"Some bizarre female mountebank," I said. "Whatever lunacy she's peddling, I'll have none of it."

Beautiful! he exclaimed.

I snorted. "If by that you mean that she resembles a mollusc more than most women, than we are in agreement."

In due course, Victor and Eleanor returned to find me restored to my proper estate. After the tears of joy and the embraces, we retired to the sitting room with the oldest bottle from my meagre cellars. As I sat, Dewey sprang into my lap and settled himself quite comfortably.

"We, too, have an announcement," Victor said, then nodded towards his bride.

"I am with child," Eleanor said, beaming. "I had suspected it for some weeks, but Dr. Samson has confirmed it." Her smile acquired a sly cast. "He says it is quite remarkably advanced for an infant conceived only two months ago."

Dewey sprang to his feet in my lap, then spread his wings and took to the air, pummeling my face with his feathers, and nearly upsetting two lamps and an antique vase in his haste to embrace Eleanor and cover her with damp Geoduck kisses of effusive congratulation, an accolade she accepted with merry laughter. I called to the servants for another bottle. This was to be a night dedicated to celebration. All was, for the moment, for the best in Tesla Hall.

That evening, after Eleanor had retired to bed, Victor and I remained in the library with a bottle of Calvados long into the night. I told Victor of my strange misadventure of the afternoon. "...and of course the most troubling part," I mused aloud, "is her awareness that ontological researches are taking place here. There must have been a lapse in our discretion somehow. But where?"

Victor silently rose and went to the bookshelf. He selected a back issue of the *Proceedings* of the Royal Academy of Speculative Metaphysics and returned to his seat, thumbing through the pages.

Then he cleared his throat and read aloud:

"'To the editors:

"'I write with regard to J. Jerome Mulbridge's 'Toward a Unified Model of Metamorphic Ontology' in your autumn issue. His subject— the action of ontological fields upon material forms—is of particular interest to myself, and I concede that the essay is exceptionally clever, and persuasively reasoned, with several substantial points of interest, one or two of which even expanded my own understanding of their subject. His presumption that such actions belong solely to the realm of theory is a common and forgivable error, which I do not begrudge him.

"'To one point, however, I must take more serious exception: Mulbridge's proposal of so-called morphic entanglement, whereby the ontological transformation of one entity produces a complimentary transition in another separate entity, is not merely offensive to common sense. It is demonstrably false. Exciting developments in my own researches have conclusively shown that no such "entanglement" does or can take place under the influence of ontological fields.

"'Unfortunately, current circumstances preclude disclosing the details of the experiments that have established this, but my word as a gentleman should suffice: morphic entanglement is utter poppycock.

"'Yours sincerely,

"'Daedalus K. Tesla, DPhil.'"

Victor looked significantly at me. "Was this the first such letter you have written on ontological science?"

"You know it was no such thing," I said. "And the ingrates only publish perhaps one in four of the remarkably informative bulletins I am kind enough to send to them."

"Perhaps if you were to refrain from deploying the phrase 'ignorant buffoon' with a liberality most writers reserve for 'it' and 'the,' you would find a readier audience."

"Does this line of argument have a purpose, other than to critique my literary style?"

"Well, you're not being terribly secretive, what?"

"Victor, the *Proceedings* of the Royal Academy of Speculative Metaphysics is a scientific journal. It isn't intended for... for females."

"Perhaps," Victor said, "no-one pointed this out to Miss Pierce."

The following morning, I arose early. My mouth was dry and my head throbbing from my unaccustomed indulgence, but I was determined to make a more substantial start of the labour that had been so thwarted the day before.

A good hour or so later, the undertaking appeared more daunting than ever as I more fully appreciated the scope of the damage done.

In time, Victor, unshaven and bleary eyed, stumbled down the stairs to greet me. With all my strength, I was tugging at a pry bar, attempting to pull apart the fused components of the morphic stabilization array, the better to assess which elements might be susceptible to repair and which had been reduced to scrap metal.

"Daedalus," he said, "whatever are you doing?"

I drew breath and resumed my efforts on the particularly stubborn categoric displacement bulb that had been resisting the bar these past several minutes. "Striving," I gasped, "to salvage what I might of my Ontological Engine." I bit back a remark about how remarkably little progress had been made during my unwilling sabbatical, my instinctive social grace suggesting to me that such an observation—however innocently intended—might be taken amiss.

"Are you in need of assistance?"

"No, no," I assured him irritably, "I've almost got it here."

"Are you certain? It looks pretty well wedged." He moved in to lay hands on the pry bar.

"Yes, I'm certain. Get out of my—"

"Let me just—"

"I think it's—"

"Have a care!"

As the displacement bulb gave way, my weight was thrown forward against the stabilizer. The bulb creaked downward for an instant, metal buckling and tearing, then dropped onto the spot where my right hand was. I jerked it away at the last possible instant and was just about to heave a sigh of relief when the heavy bulb landed squarely on my toe before rolling across the floor.

There was a moment of startling pain, then a flickering blue light and a smell of ozone. I looked about for the light's source for an instant but was seized by an intense vertiginous sensation.

When it passed, I found myself swaddled in fabric. This I wriggled out of without overmuch effort, only to find myself viewing the laboratory from an all-too-familiar perspective. The sight of Victor's astonished gape only confirmed my fears. "Daedalus, what happened?" he said.

The sheer inanity of his inquiry left me wordless for a moment. I attempted a devastating rejoinder, but of course only quacks and gurgles could be heard. I flapped my wings and stomped my feet, unleashing every vile curse and imprecation I knew, in English, Latin, and French.

In time, my fury spent itself, and I stood still, panting, my scattered feathers slowly settling to the ground about me.

"Well, this is a rather unexpected setback," Victor said at last. "I imagine you'll be wanting your pen and paper?"

I nodded my siphon. Writing, slow and painstaking as it was with the Geoduck body, was the only reliable means of direct communication available to me. And now, with Dewey likewise transformed, I would lack even the services of a translator.

Victor extended his arm to me, offering it as a perch for the trek to the library, but I shook my siphon in refusal; the indignity would have been too much to bear. Instead, I made my way to the staircase, and painstakingly clambered up first one stair, then the next.

In the dining room, Hubert and Louise were darting about in a state of considerable agitation. On the floor, three plates of eggs, beans, and toast lay half-eaten.

When they sighted me, they rushed forward, both quacking furiously. *One at a time,* I quacked at them. *I can barely understand your infernal honking when you speak one at a time, much less simultaneously.*

They subsided, then Louise resumed, quacking at a furious pace. Dewey, I heard repeatedly, and human, and once, incongruously, naked.

Yes, yes, I quacked impatiently. Dewey, your sibling who was, for a time, human. Where is he?

For once, the answer was clear.

Sofa, they both said.

The sofa was conspicuously empty, but I nonetheless flew onto its back, and looked behind. A blond youth crouched there, nude save for a pillow clutched over his genitals.

What the devil do you think you are doing, Dewey? I quacked, for it was indeed he.

"I changed back," Dewey said shamefacedly, "and you said I shouldn't be seen with my clothes off, so I hid." He looked at me in plaintive appeal. "I didn't mean to change! Truly!"

Never fear, I answered. Whatever caused it, it is perhaps for the best anyway. Now go get dressed. I have need of your services.

He sprang up and cast the pillow aside. "Thank you, Uncle Daedalus! You are very kind to me!" he said, then ran off upstairs.

Hubert and Louise had resumed their meal, and were placidly rooting about in their baked beans. Victor was looking after Dewey's pert retreating buttocks. "He really is a remarkably well-put-together lad," he said quietly.

Crisis! I quacked indignantly to all present. Does no-one recall that your master is in crisis?

None so much as glanced in my direction.

The following day found me in the basement with ever-patient Dewey. "Uncle," he said plaintively, "is this really necessary?"

I have no notion, I quacked to him. If you have an alternate suggestion as to how I might trigger further transformation, I am all... and then trailed off into morose silence as my dearth of even such humble appendages as a pair of ears was driven vividly home to me.

I ruffled my feathers and turned myself once more to the business at hand. A bit more to the left this time, I directed him, and drop it from a somewhat greater height.

"Must I, Uncle? It pains you so!"

I fixed him with a withering glare, or attempted to. My lack of anything resembling a face would have left the gesture ineffectual with most humans, but Dewey cringed as if struck, the bulb dropping from his hand. I felt a twinge of remorse at his hard treatment, obliterated a moment later by the wash of blinding pain as the massive glass globe struck my toes for the fourth time that morning.

As my hopping and cursing subsided, I heard the crunching of gravel on the drive-way without. Victor had taken the coach into town that morning, and was now evidently returned.

I confess—my will faltered. My dread of the next such impact overcame my scientific resolve and even my craving for liberation and drove me to welcome the distraction of Victor's arrival. I dashed for the door, arriving before he entered, keen, for once, to hear his gossip of the goings-on in the village of —————shire.

Victor nodded at me as he entered. "Daedalus, old fellow. I had the most remarkable—" then he interrupted himself. "Whatever happened to your foot? It wasn't nearly so bad this morning."

I shook my nozzle impatiently. Even had he been able to apprehend my speech, I would still have been reluctant to discuss the morning's tiresome labor.

Blessedly, he took the hint. "At any rate, I had the most remarkably interesting conversation down in town. This woman—Miss Pierce—I do believe you may have underestimated her."

I cleared my siphon contemptuously.

"Now, hear me out, Daedalus. I know you are a sound judge of character, but you can be set in your ways. I had a most extensive discussion of our work with Miss Pierce..."

I squawked in alarm, but Victor paid it no mind at all.

"...and it turns out that she has done some substantial work in ontological theory herself, publishing under the name of Mulbridge. So I told her that we had a nice little problem in ontology on our hands and asked her up to have a look at it. I offered her a ride in the carriage, but she insisted on taking her velocipede instead, so she should be by shor—" here he glanced through the open doorway. "In fact, here she comes now."

I was choking with horror, imagining that smug little androgyne cackling with schadenfreude as she surveyed my present humiliation. Blessedly, Dewey appeared in the doorway at just that moment.

I spoke to him rapidly, appending a stern admonition to translate—for once—literally.

Dewey blanched and swallowed loudly. "Uncle Daedalus says... if you reveal his transformation to Miss Pierce, he will... never forgive you," he said with visible reluctance.

"But—" Victor said. "Then what am I to—"

At that moment, Minerva Pierce strode in, if anything more flushed and disheveled than last I had seen her, carrying a single large, battered Gladstone bag.

"Hullo, Victor," she called. "The roads were beastly, but no match for my new-style pneumatic—"

She stopped dead as her eyes fell on me. I was seized by the urge to hide myself, but it was clearly too late for such a thing now. "What on earth is this?" she said. "I've never seen such a creature."

"This is... er... Oswald," Victor extemporized. "Daedalus has several rare... eh... Argentine lake ducks that he has imported at great cost from... um...."

His frantic improvisation trailed off.

"Argentina?" Miss Pierce prompted.

"Just so. Awfully clever little fellow. Truly part of the household."

"What a remarkable animal!" she said. She slowly set down her bags and crouched before me, extending her hand palm-out as if I were a dog. "Hullo there, Oswald," she said softly.

By instinct, I fluffed my feathers and spread my wings. From my extended siphon came a loud, menacing hiss.

Miss Pierce backed off gratifyingly at the sound. "Nervous fellow, eh?" she said to Victor.

"He may take a while to get used to you," Victor said, "but I'm sure he'll come around."

"And who is this handsome lad?" Miss Pierce said, looking at Dewey.

"I beg your pardon," Victor said. "This is my nephew, Dewey Panopea. He, too is a student of ontological science, and has been assisting with our research."

"Does he speak?"

I noticed then for the first time that Dewey's visage was quite crimson. He nodded furiously, then, appearing to realize that a demonstration was called for, squeaked, "Yes!" in a strangled tone, and managed—improbably—to darken another hue. Darting his eyes between Victor and Miss Pierce, he suddenly turned and ran from the room in a panic.

Our visitor arched her eyebrows at this mysterious display. "I seem to be making quite an impression. This Dewey isn't in any degree related to Oswald, is he?"

Now it was Victor's turn to blush and stammer, caught flat-footed by this uncanny display of perspicuity.

"Jest, Victor," she said after a time. "I spoke in jest."

"Oh!" He laughed wanly. "No, certainly not. One is human, the other is... er... a duck sort of creature. Clearly impossible, yes."

There was a brief uneasy silence.

"But you had a problem in ontological theory you wished to show me," she said at last.

"In ontological engineering," Victor corrected her.

She cocked an eyebrow skeptically. "Ontological fields are a theoretical construct. Are you actually claiming that you can generate them in the laboratory?"

"Well, no," Victor allowed. "The machine is broken, you see. But old Daedalus, he had it working beautifully before... the accident."

Her mouth turned down a bit at the mention of my name. "Well, I must say: if he is so awfully clever, I am inclined to allow him his own labour without my interference."

"Ah, yes," Victor said. "You met him yesterday, did you not?"

"I had that honour," she said icily.

"Oh, you mustn't mind Daedalus's little ways. We ordinary mortals must make allowances for the eccentricities of genius."

Her expression failed to thaw.

"Where is the great man, anyway?" she asked. "I was surprised not to find him at the end of your drive, brandishing a pike against intruders."

"Urgent business has called him away," said Victor vaguely. "A most unfortunate matter. Hopefully, he shall return shortly, but for the time, it is uncertain. Look: come on down to the laboratory—"

I let out an involuntary squawk of outrage. Victor glared at me for a scant instant. I glared right back, or attempted to; I have no idea if the gesture was in any wise recognizable.

"Come on down to the laboratory," Victor resumed, "have a look at the equipment, see if you have any ideas."

I was indignant that my labours were to be displayed to this person, but I held my siphon high as I strode away from the conversation. If my privacy was to be wrested from me thus, I would at least strive to retain some vestige of my dignity, and not stand helplessly by while my life's work was employed as a dumb-show for mendicants.

Alone, I wandered the corridors of Tesla Hall, brooding on my misfortune. In time, I blundered upon Eleanor. "Good afternoon, Mr. Tesla!" she said brightly, then started in realization.

"Oh, you poor thing, you've had a relapse!" She knelt beside me to examine me in concern. I must say, it was a relief to see someone taking my predicament seriously. "And what happened to your dear little foot?" she then asked.

I shook my siphon impatiently. The topic remained quite as sore as the appendage in question.

"Ah, Daedalus," the new Mrs. Dalrymple sighed, "if it is any comfort, you do make rather a handsome Geoduck."

As she spoke, she gently stroked along the length of my siphon, her soft fingers producing powerful sensations along my bare, wrinkled skin. I found myself shivering slightly under her touch.

"The time in London was lovely, but it was awfully lonely just Victor and me," she said softly. "I have been looking forward to having my dear friends about me again."

She leaned down and kissed me softly on the top of my siphon.

Her breath seemed at that moment unutterably sweet, full of thrilling promise. I felt the heat rising from her skin, causing my own to prickle and warm in sympathy. My Geoduck senses, attuned to detect the immaterial substance of human arousal itself, caused her to fairly glow with a thrilling radiance. I could see her skin flush and her eyes sparkle as my prehensile siphon swelled beneath her hand, thick-

ening and lengthening slightly as its wrinkles smoothed and its lim-
berness gave way to near rigidity.

At that moment, Dewey appeared at the end of the corridor.
"Uncle," he said, "is Miss Pierce still—"

His voice broke the spell of Eleanor's intoxicating proximity, and I
sprang into the air, flying gracelessly towards the shelter of my nephew
and the relief from temptation that he appeared to offer. He held out
his arms for me to land on, then attempted to stroke me soothingly
once I had perched. Another overwhelming wave of unwelcome pleasure overtook me. DON'T, I squawked, and he withdrew his hand apolo-
getically.

A moment later, I was fairly crushed between two bosoms as
Eleanor embraced Dewey, peppering his face with affectionate kisses.
"Oh, Dewey, dear boy! How I have missed you!" she exclaimed.

It would perhaps be best to explain at this juncture that Eleanor is
endowed by Nature with a temperament warm and generous almost
to a fault, a quality which has served only to endear her the further to
her husband, who, secure in her affections, permits her the greatest
freedom in what other enjoyments she pursues.

In this case, however, the pursuit offered little enough sport, with
the game fairly caught ere the first horn had been blown. Seducing
my nephew is no great challenge for near any biped with a mind to
do so, and Dewey's acquaintance with Mrs. Dalrymple had been of the
most intimate sort since before his elevation to the human race.

"Eleanor," he gasped, "your kisses make me quite giddy."

"Come, Dewey," she answered, taking him firmly by the hand, "let
us waste no time in renewing our friendship."

Wherewith, she pulled him, stumbling, in the direction of her and
Victor's bedroom. I struggled to free myself from his grasp, but he
had apparently been rendered insensible to my very existence.

In a moment she had dragged him into the room and was prod-
ding him towards the bed. *Release me this very instant!* I quacked, and he
absentmindedly complied, tumbling me painfully to the floor just as
the door swung shut behind Eleanor's impatiently flung heel.

The pair fell one way while I ran the other, they collapsing onto the
bed in a frantic embrace, myself hastening in the vain hope that the

door might somehow have failed to latch.

No such luck was to be had. I looked around, and already Eleanor had thrown her skirt up about her waist and nimbly climbed Dewey's recumbent form to press his unresisting face against her furry motte.

The doorknob, Dewey, I quacked with little hope, but indeed Eleanor's thighs had so muffled all sound that he showed not the slightest sign of having heard me.

I decided to look about for another means of escape but found myself rooted to the spot, transfixed by the sight of Mrs. Dalrymple's elegant stockinged calves and exquisitely soft pale thighs, her ample bottom rotating slowly over Dewey's trapped face. Her expressions likewise held my attention as they moved from gentle pleasure to fierce ardour, and thence to one more lost and abstracted, her mouth falling open and her eyes fluttering nearly shut as her cries rose in pitch and timbre.

Dewey's hands had meanwhile not been idle, one caressing the smooth expanse of Eleanor's bottom, while the other unfastened his trousers to release his slender pego, red and rigid, already slick with the anticipatory fluid he produced in such extraordinary abundance.

Eleanor leaned forward now, like a jockey urging his steed to greater efforts, chewing on the knuckles of one hand to stifle her screams of delight until she convulsed with pleasure, and then she dismounted unsteadily, revealing Dewey's red and shining face, his golden hair hopelessly tousled by her grasping fingers.

Doorknob, I quacked forlornly, but my voice was choked by the intensity of the emotions that suffused me, and neither Dewey nor Eleanor gave any sign of having heard me.

With practiced hands, Dewey assisted Eleanor in removing her gown and stays, and in minutes she stood quite perfectly naked in the centre of the room. Her gravidity had just begun to work its changes on her body. Her bosom had swelled a bit, her aureoles darkening from a delicate pink to a Capuchin brown. Her belly had acquired a subtle convexity since last I had seen it. The breath caught in my siphon to behold her; the blood pounded in my nozzle.

Dewey, too, had divested himself of his clothes by this time, and she swarmed upon him, running her face over his near-hairless chest, his flat belly. His rubicund affair left glistening trails across her face as she rubbed it over her cheeks before taking it into her mouth for a moment of exquisite suction that caused him to gasp and arch his back.

Then she rolled off of him, rising to her hands and knees facing me, then waggling her hips in provocative invitation. Dewey crouched behind her, and I could read the moment of penetration in their intent expressions more clearly than if I had seen it directly.

"Oh, Eleanor," Dewey groaned, as he pressed his hips against hers, "how I have missed you."

"And I you, dear Dewey," Eleanor answered. "Faster, I pray you. I need your dear cock so!"

Dewey complied, accelerating his thrusts so that Eleanor's soft bosoms shook bewitchingly. She raised up her shoulders the better to counterbalance his forceful pounding, and her eyes fell upon myself, yet standing transfixed in front of the door.

"Daedalus," she called out between gasps, "come join us!"

I shook my siphon in absolute refusal. But howsoever unwilling the spirit, the flesh was yet weak, and my rebellious legs took step after step towards the shaking bed. Frozen at its foot, I stood a time, trembling with thwarted desire, as Eleanor cradled her head in her arms, her whole body shaking at each thrust from the slender lad behind her. Finally, my resistance crumbled, and I flapped up to the foot of the bed. Both Dewey and Eleanor paused in their thrusting to smile welcomingly at me, and Eleanor reached out her hand and gripped my siphon, squeezing with a force I might otherwise have expected to be painful, but which at that moment sent the most exquisite pleasure rushing through me.

By that grip, she dragged me forward, and she ran her exquisitely hot and moist tongue over the tip of my nozzle, hungrily lapping up the slick fluid that by now ran down as copiously as if I were Dewey himself. Months of pent-up desire rose within me like Leviathan from his pelagic trench.

As Dewey redoubled the speed of his thrusts, her sharp little teeth nipped at my shaft, serving only to add piquancy to the pleasure suffusing my form.

Eleanor was sucking now at the tip of my siphon, enclosing me utterly in darkness, warmth, and exquisite pressure.

Faintly, from outside, I heard Dewey crying out as he neared his crisis. Eleanor's mouth released my siphon for an instant, and I drew in a great gasping breath, not realizing that I had been holding it. I smelled arousal—male, female, and Geoduck—sweat, lavender powder, and... ozone? "I spend!" Dewey gasped, and a flickering blue radiance filled the room. *Not now! I quacked.*

For a single moment the blue lightning played over Dewey's rapidly-contracting form. I sprang away, but the glow leapt from him to me, and I found myself nude and fully human, tumbling off the foot of the bed.

❧

"Ouch," I said.

Then, "Eureka!" I sprang to my feet. "Morphic entanglement!" I exclaimed. "I always suspected it was possible. Dewey, don't you see?"

Dewey was slumped on his back, carapace heaving as his nozzle panted for breath. He raised his siphon now in tepid curiosity.

"Sufficient mental excitation in either one of us can cause both to—erm—oh..."

Standing, my rigid member had protruded over the bed, and Eleanor had taken the opportunity to take it in her mouth.

With effort, I gathered my thoughts to speak once more. "Eleanor, this is an extraordinary realization I have reached. Have you no sense of proportion at all?"

She removed her mouth from my affair, immediately replacing it with a gripping hand. "I most certainly do," she answered heatedly, and resumed her suction upon my affair.

My body shouted its assent to her logic, my back arching under her skillful ministrations, but compared to the terrible compulsions of the Geoduck form, it was relatively easy to extract myself from her grip with an apologetic shake of my head.

"This new datum makes attending to my equilibrium more crucial then ever," I told her, not without regret. "I'm certain that, given a few minutes rest, Dewey will be capable of attending to your needs as ably as ever."

"Neglect me in my time of need, Daedalus, and you may yet regret it," Eleanor said resentfully.

"I do already, my dear. I do already." And with those words, I operated the previously inaccessible doorknob and made a dash for my own bedroom to find suitable clothes to change into.

A few minutes later, I entered the sitting room from the upstairs landing, only to find Victor and Miss Pierce doing likewise from the laboratory.

"Mr. Tesla!" the woman said upon sighting me. She strode up to me, seized my hand in both of her own, and shook it furiously. "I must thank you from the very bottom of my heart!"

"Must you?" I said, befuddled, my whole body shaking from the force of the small woman's vigourous movements.

"Your Ontological Engine," she said, "is one of the most beautiful things I have ever beheld!"

"Oh! Well, it—"

"The genius of the design! The elegance! The sheer intellectual audacity!"

I found myself blushing a bit at this unexpected onslaught of praise. "Well, it's just a prototype, really...."

"It is an honour—an honour, sir—just to witness a work that so incalculably advances the science of ontology. Your assistant believed that I might be of assistance on this magnificent project, and I dare suspect he might be correct. But I wouldn't dare lay hands on such a masterpiece without its creator's permission."

There was a moment's silence before I realized that some response was here called for.

"Well, yes," I said at last. "I'm certain you will be quite an asset to the endeavour."

Again she seized my hand, again she pumped it frantically, with even more tooth-rattling vigour than before. "You won't regret it, sir!

I'll just get my tools and go right to work!" She dashed out of the room and could be seen through the front window removing further bags precariously fastened to her velocipede.

"You know, Victor," I said, "I do believe you may have underestimated this Miss Pierce. She seems quite a remarkably clever individual."

The weeks that followed presented distinctive challenges along several axes. For the Dalrymples, the introduction of a person not initiated into the amatory freedom that had previously characterized the household required a frustrating curtailing of their habitual debauches. Nonetheless, both seemed to take pleasure in her company and never spoke a word of complaint to me about her presence.

For myself, when I was in human form, the period was reminiscent in some ways of the era when I had first taken Victor on as my assistant, characterized by an increased productivity of my labours on the one hand and the necessity of elision and even prevarication on the other, as Miss Pierce's probing questions about the power source for my engines touched on matters I was not prepared to discuss with her.

However, whenever I was "called away on urgent errands of unforeseeable duration," the situation was less comfortable. Whereas, previously, I had insisted on maintaining my human dignity, continuing to sleep in my own bed and eating at table with the others (to the amazement and consternation of the servants), I now was compelled to play the part of Oswald, taking my meals and my repose with Hubert and Louise, who were glad enough of the extra company, which served to compensate them in part for the curtailing of their activities with Eleanor and Victor.

We soon learned to recognize the symptoms of an impending transformation and hasten to privacy, but not without perilous close calls and a number of socially awkward abrupt withdrawals.

When in Geoduck form, Dewey took to following our lady engineer about like a puppy, rubbing against her limbs and springing into her lap whene'er she sat.

In human form, his adoration was less naked, but no less pronounced, as he hastened to run errands for her pleasure and comfort,
and stammeringly endeavoured to make conversation with her. She in
turn did nothing to discourage his preoccupation, seeming to take a
certain pleasure in his obvious devotion.

On the whole, however, Miss Pierce seemed oblivious to anything
but the labours at hand. She conversed of little but ontological theory
at meals, spending long hours building, riveting, soldering, and carefully testing my rebuilt Ontological Engine.

What little waking leisure she allowed herself she largely spent
keeping company with Eleanor whilst the latter laboured at her sewing
and embroidery in the sitting room. This refreshingly feminine pursuit was marred only by her habit of smoking small, pungent cheroots
as she conversed with the young mother-to-be.

One evening, Victor inquired of me how long I intended to keep
Miss Pierce in the dark about the erotic aspects of my researches.

"Indefinitely," I told him. "It is clear that Miss Pierce possesses a
particularly prudish disposition and would certainly be indignant at
any whiff of our inquiry into the nature and effects of vital fluids."

Sly Fortuna saw fit to locate me in the library the very next morn-
ing, where I was trying to locate one memorable passage in Moriarty's
Dynamics of an Asteroid. I had been paging through for some time when
I heard footsteps and voices from the next room.

Where ordinary speech would have gone ignored, the trivia of
feminine intercourse interesting me not at all, the hushed and furtive
tones from the next room excited my voracious curiosity, and I crept
to the doorway to listen.

"Miss Pierce, how bold you are!" Eleanor gasped.

"Nonsense," came the reply, "I am by nature as meek a creature as
you can find in all of England. It is only your beauty that inspires me
to boldness and compels me to ask—to beg—you for another kiss."

Could this be? Was this person seducing members of my own
household under my very nose?

"Oh," said Eleanor, "I—" but the remainder of her sentence was
muffled.

"It's just between us girls, and you know there can be no harm in that," Pierce coaxed. Muffled moans and sighs sounded together in an intricate duet.

"Oh, that is lovely," sighed Eleanor. "I've never had a woman make love to me before, unless of course you count Lou—" she caught herself at the last moment before a potentially shocking disclosure. "—ella. My old schoolmate."

"Ah, school days," Miss Pierce said. "After hours in the dormitory, hands searching blindly 'neath one another's nightgowns...." There was a rustling sound.

"Oh!"

"Happy memories, indeed."

"Oh, you make me quiver, Minerva!"

"And you me," Miss Pierce was saying. "Your dear little cunny is so hot, the fur upon it is so soft!"

I was quivering myself by this time. That this woman had so deluded us all, forcing us to tiptoe about like mice in my own ancestral house, while secretly scheming her own debauches. Oh, it galled!

But, like Prince Hamlet, I had hesitated too long before striking my blow. I count myself a man of not-inconsiderable force of will, but even I hesitated to unleash the fury that is Eleanor Dalrymple, frustrated in love. I would bide my time until she had taken her pleasure.

"Tell me," Miss Pierce was saying, "did Louella ever initiate you into the delights of *Aphrodite's kiss?*"

"Why, whatever do you mean?" Eleanor said, playing the ingenue with marvelous conviction.

"Here, recline for a moment on the chaise, and I shall demonstrate."

There was a further rustling, then Eleanor said, "Oh, surely you do not mean to, to kiss my—Oh, my goodness, how exquisite!"

Miss Pierce's voice was barely audible, muffled as it was by layers of crinoline; "Hush" and "be heard" were all I caught.

"Oh," sighed Eleanor more quietly, "I have never felt anything so— a little to the left if you please. Yes, just so—anything so utterly marvelous. What pleasure you give me, Minerva!"

Under the cover of this distracting activity, I crept into the room, finding the tableau much as I had anticipated, Eleanor recumbent, one limb thrown up over the back of the chaise, Miss Pierce in a black and yellow sailor suit that caused her vividly to evoke the bee, diligently harvesting his honey from the indolent flowers.

As I entered, Eleanor favoured me with a cheery smile, her eyes lingering appraising upon the bulge in my trousers, before shutting them the better to turn her attention to the sensations that now suffused her form.

"Oh, what is this that is happening to me," Eleanor whispered heatedly, "what do you make me do?"

She gritted her teeth against the cries that strove to escape, then collapsed, panting. A moment later, Miss Pierce disentangled herself from Eleanor's numerous skirts, then made as if to embrace the exhausted girl.

Ere that tender scene could commence, however, I cleared my throat, and Miss Pierce sprang to her feet, yelping in startlement.

I do confess, it was not ungratifying to firmly have the better of this vexing person—an intellect not incomparable to my own, crammed perversely into a nominally female form.

"I feed you," I said, "I house you, I take you into my very home, I share with you the secrets of Ontological Engineering, and how is my generosity repaid?"

Miss Pierce's flushed and shining face was tilted up with a look of fierce defiance, though her gaze flickered downward repeatedly.

"My so-called engineer turns out to be naught but a triband!"

"Tribade," she said. I realized that her glance, like Eleanor's, was noting the erection that still distended my clothes. My sense of control of the situation was slipping rapidly.

"Ah, very well, cover your filthy lies with pedantry!" I shouted.

"I have lied to you about nothing," she said with a cold fury. "You, on the other hand, have told me a great deal about ontological engines powered by coal and steam, every word of which is the most perfect horse-shite."

I clenched my fists in fury at her underhanded riposte, and opened my mouth to deliver a scathing reply, when a horridly familiar sensation washed over me. I turned to flee the room, but it was too late.

When I had managed to extract myself from my clothes, Miss Pierce stood rooted to the spot. "Fascinating!" she exclaimed. "Vitalistically triggered morphic instability! I never dreamed...."

Eleanor, still reclining upon the divan with a dreamy smile, spoke up: "Now, Daedalus. You mustn't allow yourself to become so agitated. Look what has happened!"

"He remains sentient in this form?" Miss Pierce said wonderingly. "How marvelous! This demands further investigation."

She took a step towards me, and I backed towards the door, visions of vivisection wrenching a ferocious hiss from my siphon.

Another step, and I turned and ran, wings pumping madly, Miss Pierce in hot pursuit. In the sitting room, I found no further doors open, and sprang behind the sofa, determined to hide myself, or, failing that, to make a last desperate stand there. The position, however, turned out to be already occupied by my opposite number, who had once again found himself abruptly nude and human in the sitting-room.

"Dewey," Miss Pierce said, upon finding us there, "I do not mean to pry, but I cannot help but wonder why you are entirely devoid of— But of course! Morphic entanglement! How utterly marvelous."

Dewey stood, and, recollecting his nudity, snatched me up for use as a makeshift shield for his genitals. I squawked at this indignity, flapping my wings to no avail.

Tell that abominable woman that her employment here is terminated! I quacked to Dewey.

He looked down at me, aghast.

"Can you understand his speech?" Miss Pierce said.

"No, no," he said at once. "Not in the least!"

Have you quite lost your mind, Dewey? I quacked indignantly. *Of course you can understand me.*

Miss Pierce said, "Well, he is most probably trying to give me the sack."

Even this ridiculous woman is able to grasp my meaning. Surely your senses have not utterly abandoned you.

"Oh!" Dewey looked like he might be about to cry. "I can't imagine that Uncle Daedalus would say something so... so horrid."

"If I am correct, it is a bit of a shame." Miss Pierce said. "I should have liked an opportunity to test out my design for a Morphic Decoupler. It would have been a nice project to attempt to undo the entanglement that has occurred between the two of you.... Still, it is best I go start packing." She turned to leave.

DO NOT LET THAT WOMAN LEAVE THIS HOUSE! I quacked.

"Uncle Daedalus requests that you stay with us a while yet," Dewey said.

Miss Pierce turned once more, with a look of abominable satisfaction upon her face. "I do like this household," she said, "You are all such wonderfully bad liars."

There was a truce, then, between us, but an armed one. She largely abandoned work on the Engine to begin construction of her proposed Decoupler—at a renegotiated extortionate wage. We thus spent many a long day in the laboratory, working in parallel, a frosty silence largely prevailing. From time to time the intoxication of a particularly fine point of theory or execution would distract us enough that we would chatter like old friends for a time, but then we would remember ourselves and resume our wary stances. Victor aided us both with cheery equanimity, while Dewey strove to assist on Miss Pierce's project, but proved so flustered by her close proximity that in time she primarily employed him in errands that kept him well out of the laboratory.

She continued to sit with Eleanor at her sewing. I offered to Victor to arrange suitable chaperonage, but he failed to grasp its necessity. Nonetheless, I made a point of dropping in from time to time and was pleased to see that Miss Pierce had herself taken up—of all things—a sewing project of her own. I attempted to mend fences between us and asked after the nature of the project, but she only smiled slyly and told me that it was "a work in progress."

On one topic, however, she was all too voluble. She peppered me incessantly with questions about the true power source for the Engine.

"Never you mind that," I told her. "You concern yourself with building the Decoupler, and I shall provide the power." Her persistence was remarkable. She ventured queries harsh, sly, gentle, frank, menacing, comradely, even—clumsily—flirtatious; but I was resolute—I did not wish to entrust this woman with my most potent secrets.

Miss Pierce, keen to learn how I had mustered sufficient ontological energies to fabricate the Geoducks, did not content herself with interrogating only my own person. Eleanor, Victor, and Dewey also came in for persistent questioning, and I am far from certain that she did not attempt to extract information from Hubert and Louise as well.

∾

Now, dear reader, I must beg your indulgence as I set forth events whose full details were not revealed to me until a later time. Extensive subsequent interviews with Dewey produced the fuller picture of the beginnings of that remarkable evening which I shall now relate.

Rummaging about in the laboratory, Miss Pierce found the Collection Stand, the Amatory Circlet, and their associated control bank. Her deductive powers led her to conclude that they were designed to somehow harness a living creature to serve as the ontological dynamo, but beyond that, her vision would not reach.

Accordingly, a few words in Dewey's siphon prevailed upon him to secretly meet her at midnight at the door to the laboratory. Clad only in her night-clothes, she carried Dewey cradled in one arm, while the other gripped her sewing project, creeping furtively down the creaking basement stairs.

Dewey, overwhelmed by excitement at this assignation, was secreting the fluid that gave him his name with characteristic copiousness.

"Look at you, Dewey," she said teasingly, dabbing at the underside of his siphon with a handkerchief, "what a messy creature you are!" As his secretions were absorbed into the skin of her hand, her colour heightened noticeably, and the tempo of her breathing altered. "You know, I confess that once I found you quite the ugly little fellow in this form, but now I see you to be the dearest little creature in all the world!"

Dewey wriggled in Miss Pierce's arms at this praise, so suffused with delight that a faint crackle of blue energy could be seen about the base of his siphon.

By this time she was igniting the gaslights in the basement laboratory, whereby Dewey beheld the collection platform, still scorched and blackened, a small woody protrusion marking the spot where a minute cocoanut palm had sprouted during a prior experiment with ontological forces. Only now the collection circuit was harnessed not to my massive Ontological Engine, but to Miss Pierce's more modestly-proportioned Morphic Decoupler.

He betrayed some agitation as she carried him to the collection platform, but she spoke to him soothingly: "I am so very glad that you agreed to meet me here. I have been wishing to spend some time with you in private." Her hand stroked the sensitive spot where his siphon met his shell in such a manner that he only sighed with pleasure as she placed him gently upon the platform, and he noticed nothing amiss until twin clicks alerted him to her having fastened the manacles about his legs.

Dewey quacked in dismay and shook his legs, rattling the chains; but there was little to be done now.

"I wouldn't want you to betray any confidences," she said conversationally, striding to the Decoupler, "but if you simply assist me to discover how to use these devices for myself, your innocence will remain untarnished." She activated the device, and a faint, deep hum suffused the laboratory.

She leaned down until her lips were scant inches from Dewey's panting nozzle. "And you do wish to assist me, do you not?" Torn agonizingly between loyalty and desire, Dewey made not a sound.

She threaded the metallic circlet along the length of Dewey's siphon until it rested upon his shell like a gleaming cravat, and a faint green radiance began to flicker along the Decoupler. Her eyes widened in delight. "Already we make progress," she exclaimed. She scrutinized the meters on the amatory condenser, then turned back to the helplessly bound Geoduck.

"Now it remains only to figure out how to extract more usable quantities of these emanations from you. Is there some state in which this energy is produced more copiously?"

Dewey was mute.

"Come, Dewey. There is a key, and I would have it. Anger, slumber, mirth? Pain?"

He whimpered a little at this last, and there was a faint crackling noise as the radiance about the Decoupler fitfully increased. The hum from the device rose a note or two on the scale.

Miss Pierce sighed and shook her head. "Oh, I can play the villain well enough. But I haven't the fortitude for any real cruelty to you, dear Dewey." She took my nephew to her bosom and stroked his siphon soothingly. "If you truly wish, I shall release you this very instant."

Separated from her yielding flesh by a single layer of fabric, his acutely sensitive siphon massaged by her hot, calloused fingers, battered by a succession of unnamable emotions, Dewey whimpered once more, as his siphon began to swell and distend. Visible tendrils of green lightning now formed a radiant halo around the Morphic Decoupler.

Miss Pierce's eyes widened at this pyrotechnic display, then she looked back at Dewey with wild surmise.

"Dewey, my stroking—" her touch on his siphon was now firmer, steadier. "—it gives you pleasure, does it not?"

Fearing that the secret was lost, Dewey shook his nozzle wildly, but it was too late. She leaned down and ran her soft cheeks over the puckered end of his siphon, and the throb of the Decoupler rose to a sustained pulsating whine as the green radiance cast an unearthly light across the entire laboratory.

Upstairs, I sat bolt upright in bed. I looked about, uncertain what had rudely jerked me out of my slumber, and in the darkness of my bedroom, the faintest possible sparks of green light could be seen rising from my skin. An instant later, I detected a distant mechanical hum. I threw on my dressing-gown and rushed down-stairs.

When I threw open the door that led to the laboratory, I could see Dewey in Miss Pierce's power, her hand by now squeezing his siphon with a slow, firm, practiced stroke that had him shuddering and gurgling with helpless delight and exuding fluid from his nozzle so copiously that her arm gleamed with moisture quite to the elbow.

She turned at the sound of my arrival, her expression eerie and feral in the stark green light.

"Mr. Tesla," she said, "I supposed you might make an appearance." Meanwhile, the stroking of Dewey's siphon continued unabated.

"You monster!" I cried. "What have you done to poor Dewey?"

"I thought you would pleased to see me cured of my tribadism," she taunted me. "Not that I wouldn't enjoy doing the same to Eleanor in this very spot."

Clearly talk was not to avail against this madwoman. Action would have to suffice. "Fear not, Dewey! I shall save you," I cried out, and made my way down the stairs.

Miss Pierce turned to Dewey and tightened her grip on his siphon. "Spend, Dewey," she said softly. "Spend for me now," and she leaned down and ran her tongue from the tip of his nozzle down the length of his siphon to the tender spot where it met his shell.

Dewey squealed and shuddered, his siphon standing as rigid as a flagpole, blue and green sparks crackling along its length. Coolly, Miss Pierce adjusted his angle, and as I came around her infernal device, prepared to employ whatever force was necessary, I was struck in the chest by a gout of thick, hot fluid.

For an instant, I beheld Dewey transforming before the change struck me as well.

❧

I struggled to free myself from my dressing-gown but found that I was being lifted, bundled into the fabric of the gown so that I was caught as truly as any netted game.

"Oh, Miss Pierce," came Dewey's muffled voice. "Pray be gentle with Uncle Daedalus! He does mean well."

"Never fear, dear one," said that abominable woman. "And you really must call me Minerva, now that we are such good friends. All I intend to do to your uncle is to allow him to exercise his masculine privilege."

Her hands reached into my dressing-gown and gripped me firmly.

I was drawn out, my wings held tight to my shell, and thrust into a tangle of fabric, the purpose of which was unclear, but which I recognized at once as Miss Pierce's sewing project on which she had been so very coy. Ribbons tightened on either side, and I found myself held fast, my wings pinned in place.

Miss Pierce held me aloft to gaze appraisingly at my curious straitjacket, and my Geoduck senses beheld a positive whirlwind of amatory force swirling about both herself and the nude youth upon the Collection Stand, whose previous climax had apparently not sufficed to satisfy his appetites.

Then, quite unexpectedly, she removed her nightgown, leaving herself entirely nude. Her small breasts, nipples tight in the laboratory's cool air, substantial thighs, and broad pubic mound held my gaze even in these unwelcome circumstances, the penumbra of excitement about her acting upon me like an irresistible aroma. She moved me from side to side in her hands, and my siphon shifted to track her mons. "Your hostility seems to be dissipating, Dr. Tesla," she said. "Pray, don't give up too fast. It will sap so much of the pleasure from your conquest."

Then she flipped me onto my back and commenced to step into other portions of the assemblage that held me fast, so that we now both wore the same garment. Inverted and helpless, I could make her out only by craning my siphon. She bestrode me now, an obscene colossus, and pulled me against her swollen labia, the moist heat of her flesh sending an erotic charge through me that so stiffened my siphon that I could scarce turn to look at her.

Straps were tightened once more, and her hand released me. I was held in place betwixt her thighs entirely by her infernal device, protruding from her groin like some bizarre figurehead, my siphon waving from side to side in frantic protest. Furiously I attempted to kick at her, eliciting only an appreciative chuckle. "Oh, that feels lovely," she said with warm malice. "Pray do that quite as much as you should wish."

Then she turned her attention back to Dewey, who was sitting up now, watching the proceedings with bafflement and concern.

She posed, presenting herself (our selves!) in profile for his scrutiny. "What do you think, Dewey?" she said. "Not the most elegant dildoe I ever have worn, but it has a certain distinctive charm, do you not think?"

"Dildoe...?" said Dewey.

"Why, yes," said Miss Pierce, walking slowly towards him. "I have very much been wishing to fuck you, Dewey." She took hold of me, midway along my siphon, and squeezed, sending waves of unwelcome pleasure along its length. My nozzle swung desperately from side to side, but the shaft was held fast. "And now I shall. With the kind assistance of your uncle."

Dewey gasped at the obscenity. "To fuck me? But I am a man!"

"Indeed you are," she said. She was close enough now that her free hand could reach out and gently run her fingertips down Dewey's heaving chest. The Morphic Decoupler, which had been nearly silent for some minutes, now began once more to hum. "And a singularly lovely one."

The head of my siphon was now batting against the soft fuzz of Dewey's belly as Miss Pierce leaned in and gently, lingeringly, kissed him on the lips.

"Oh," he sighed.

"Here," Miss Pierce said, and she took one of his hands in her own, guiding it to grip my shaft as she had been doing. She held it in place as her other reached down and took Dewey's own slender phallus in its grip and began slowly to stroke. He shuddered, and his hand echoed her own motions as if operated by her will rather than his own.

"Good boy," she murmured. The pleasure of Dewey's hand on my siphon had me nearly rigid with engorgement and dabbing clear fluid on Dewey's navel.

"Now recline for me," she coaxed him, and pushed him gently onto his back, leaning forward to continue brushing her lips over his own, then lowering herself to lap, and then nip, at his tight little nipples. Dewey's grip on my siphon was broken, but now I was pressed against the hot, crinkled skin of his cods, through which could be felt the firm root of his cockstand.

"Legs up," she prompted, and in seconds his heels rested against his bottom, knees wide spread.

Miss Pierce moved down once more, so that my siphon now protruded into air, pointing at the Collection Stand, where her tongue tip was lapping the commingled fluid on Dewey's stomach. With each stroke of her hand upon his prick, another transparent bead could be seen to form and drip into the puddle there. "My goodness, how much you do produce," she said wonderingly.

"I am sorry, Miss—Minerva," Dewey stammered.

"Not at all. I foolishly neglected to bring my bottle of glycerine this evening, so you are really being quite helpful." She ran two fingers through the viscous liquid, then brought them down to press against the crease of his bottom.

"Oh," said Dewey. "I—Oh!" Miss Pierce was working her fingers in slow circles about his fundament, not yet penetrating, but making the prospect vividly central in Dewey's fuddled mind.

I attempted to recoil as she brought her other hand down to me, but there was nowhere to flee to as she gripped the base of my siphon, tugging at it in a firm milking motion. She brought the hand that had been at Dewey's anus down and caught the fluid she thus forced out of me.

This was then applied likewise to Dewey's bottom. She stood up straight, one hand between Dewey's legs. The other gripped his hair, forcing his face into direct engagement with her own.

"Are you ready?"

"Oh, Miss Pierce," he said, "I don't really know if—"

Then the breath seemed to rush out of him as one of her fingers breached the pucker of his bottom. His prick, unattended, bobbed vigourously, the head distending further and darkening in hue as the noise and radiance from the Morphic Decoupler reached a new height.

Dewey drew a gulping breath, then cried out, cries which only increased in pitch as her finger found its way, in halting motion, within him, until her knuckles were pressed against his perineum. She took hold of his prick, and his hips shuddered, frozen in conflict between the drive to thrust against the teasing hand on his cock and to hold still against the invading digit in his arse-hole.

"My goodness!" she exclaimed. "What a cunning little bottom-hole you have, dear boy. Why, I do believe it is trying to suck me in!"

"Thank you," Dewey gasped, "I do try to keep it in good condition."

Miss Pierce shook her head in wonderment, then commenced grinding her hand in slow circles against the compliant youth's sphincter, so that he squirmed against her in counterpoint to the undulations of her two hands.

The sight of that penetration had me transfixed. I could feel anticipatory fluid positively dripping down the underside of my siphon as I strained towards that bewitching intersection. A low gurgling noise came from me as my sight remained glued to Miss Pierce's finger patiently stretching the snug orifice in which it was embedded.

"Never you fear, Daedalus," my captor purred, "I have not forgotten you."

"Dewey," she said, "do you think you are ready for something a touch more... ambitious?"

Dewey looked down, eyes wide as he took in my girth and length. I tried to shake my nozzle, to speak, to struggle, but my lustful instincts drove me forward such that only a strangled gurgle could be heard.

"I don't know," Dewey said, "but I shall try."

"Brave, brave boy." She extracted her finger, and I watched his anus pulse as it re-closed, drawing ever nearer as she shuffled up to position herself between his legs.

"Legs all the way up now," she coaxed him, and Dewey obediently lofted his bare limbs until he was embracing his knees, his genitals and anus perfectly exposed.

At last my nozzle was pressed against the damp flesh of Dewey's bottom, the thin pale hair matted with anticipatory fluid. The hunger of that orifice to be penetrated poured into me, amplifying my own desire to penetrate into an intolerable craving. Faintly, in the distance, I could hear a fierce electrical crackling.

Miss Pierce thrust her hips in minute motions; I felt Dewey's sphincter press against my siphon and recede again, in intolerably teasing rhythm. I felt it start to give way, then close and resist again several times. Then I was withdrawn another inch or so. "Deep breath now, Daedalus," Miss Pierce said, and I complied without thinking.

In the next moment, unbearable gratification came as my nozzle was permitted to penetrate Dewey's bottom. Muffled, I heard his single sharp cry.

Then, barely an inch within, I was held in place. Desperately, furiously, I strove to enter further within, to penetrate as fully as my instincts demanded, working myself back and forth the scant distance my bondage allowed.

"I don't know that I have ever had a dildoe so eager for its work before," said Miss Pierce's faint amused voice.

Then I was out, in flickering green light, with just time to release my breath and draw another, before I was plunged in once more, this time thrust in so deep all outside sound was lost to me, so that all I could hear was the furious pounding of Dewey's heartbeat.

I was held nearly still once again. I kicked furiously in protest against this teasing, but could feel that the tattoo beat by my webbed feet upon her genitals was only sufficing to gratify my torturer further.

This time, when I was drawn out, I caught a glimpse of Miss Pierce's hand sliding along Dewey's rigid prick. He whimpered piteously, aching now to be penetrated once more, a sound I shamefully echoed. The whine and crackle of the Morphic Decoupler was by this time loud enough that when I was inserted once more, the quiet within Dewey's bowels was one more element of pleasure to my already-overwhelmed constitution.

Now, at last, she commenced with thrusting in earnest, and I flung my nozzle from side to side in delight, eliciting the most remarkable yips and howls from Dewey, conducted via his flesh to my hearing, my siphon being by this time buried entirely within his frantically clutching fundament.

Along my underside, pressed against Miss Pierce's genitals, I could detect not just an answering wetness and engorgement that echoed Dewey's and my own, but her arousal itself, swelling and mounting towards its own perverse climax at the strange sensations and notions of this most-unnatural position.

Once more, I found myself in cool air, throbbing green light, and an agonizing lack of sensation. Dewey was crying out with each stroke of Miss Pierce's glistening hand, while the Morphic Decoupler throbbed in perfect synchrony with his calls. "Deep breath now, Daedalus," said Miss Pierce, gasping herself. "It is time for our final ascent to the summit."

I had barely time to fill my lungs before I was savagely plunged within once more. Heat, darkness, exquisite pleasure—but the darkness now mitigated somewhat, as green flashes of light illuminated even these close quarters, leaving a sharp tingling sensation like the discharge of electricity from a Leyden jar. Buried to my shoulders in Dewey, I howled, kicking frantically with my feet, and was swallowed up in a vortex of unbearable pleasure, ejaculatory contractions turning every fibre of my body to the exquisitely misplaced mating task. I lost consciousness.

~

At some unknown hour during that night, I became a man once more. I half-awoke, naked and shivering, only a thin blanket between me and the laboratory floor's flagstones, clutching at the warm, naked bodies beside me. Curled companionably between human and Geoduck forms, I slept once more.

In the grey light of dawn, I sat bold upright. The warm back I had been so intimately curled against was that of Miss Minerva Pierce, who blinked sleepily at me. "Congratulations, Daedalus," she said. "You are decoupled."

"What?"

"The procedure was a success," she said, stretching lazily. Her motions in turn awoke Dewey, who turned his siphon towards her. "Unless I am very much mistaken (and I rarely am), you are no longer morphically entangled with that adorable young fellow you call your nephew." Dewey quacked happily at the news and nuzzled his siphon against her, which she petted affectionately.

I struggled to assimilate this datum. "I—I—I cannot endorse your methods, but if your results are as you say, you are entitled to my thanks."

She stood and bowed slightly, a rather curious sight, given her complete nudity.

"To be fully restored to myself once more.... To never have to fear another transformation.... I feel rather giddy!"

"Oh, I have no doubt you will be transforming again. I merely solved your morphic entanglement. And a pretty puzzle it was, too. The next time Dewey turns human, I fully expect you to remain un-affected. And vice versa, of course. In fact, if I am in error, simply in-form me, and I shall cheerfully refund all the wages you have paid me."

"But... how can I prevent transforming?"

As I sputtered, she was pulling on her night-gown.

"I imagine that you shall simply have to learn to control your emo-tions."

"To control—!" My fury at her smug indifference was rising rap-idly, and blue sparks popped about my temple. I clenched my fists, gritted my teeth, and drew a slow breath, struggling to master myself.

"See?" she said. "You are making progress already. Farewell, Mr. Tesla. It has been a most particular pleasure working with you, and I somehow feel certain that I shall see you again one day."

And with that, she trotted up the stairs, Dewey following at her heels, and shut the door behind her.

"Not if I see you first!" I shouted at the indifferent door, and turned into a Geoduck.

The Terminando

Chapter 1: The Ontoscaphe

My darling Eleanor,

First, know that I am well, I am safe, and I am as happy as I can be, sundered from your arms.

Of the principles and construction of the Ontoscaphe I hardly need tell you. I am all too aware that far too many of my final days and nights with you were given over to my interminable expounding upon the subject—time that might far more profitably have been spent revelling in the joys of my most exquisite and dear little wifey. Even now, my heart aches and my pulse quickens as I imagine the delights I foolishly forwent in favour of that lesser quest for knowledge and glory.

Daedalus's scornful mockery of the undertaking galled me, and I was fiercely determined to prove my mentor wrong. I apologize, my love, for my rashness then. That I should suffer for it now is only just; but that you should suffer for it as well shames me beyond measure.

As you no doubt recall, after the promising initial tests, Dewey and I were bedevilled for weeks by a thousand fine and subtle problems, taunted day to day by the ever-elusive prospect of imminent success, so that we progressed, by turns, from wild optimism to frustration and irritation to a numb sort of dogged despair, unwilling yet to surrender but no longer able to truly imagine success. I know I was no joy to live with during that time, preoccupied and foul-tempered, worrying always at the dry and dented bone of the problem in ontological engineering.

I belabour my frame of mind thus to try to grant you some insight into what transpired on that terrible day. For what seemed the thousandth time, we had gone over all the wiring and connections, reconsidered all of our theoretical calculations, made adjustments to the transporter to try to circumvent our prior errors. "Very well," I said with a sigh, "buckle up, Dewey."

We fastened ourselves into our seats, and I threw the switch providing electrickal power to the 'scaphe. We both jumped in alarm as the postulate neutralisers flickered with violet energy. A moment later, that feeble glow had spread to the destabilization frame, wreathing our strange craft in undulating streamers of radiance.

"Check the settings!" Dewey called out. Hurriedly, I did so. With too small an ontological shift, another Victor and another Dewey might be performing the same experiment; colliding ontoscaphes could be disastrous. Too great a shift might send us to a world unpeopled, perhaps with conditions inimical to human life.

The dials were what we optimistically hoped to be in that median zone, as much as could be discerned with an untested device. I looked them over frantically as the whine of the engine increased in pitch. Strange nameless colours jumped and played across the fittings of the Ontoscaphe.

Suddenly light was steaming in through the viewport. I looked out and saw that we rested now in a sunlit meadow, whose merry sunshine dwarfed the feeble artificial glow of our ontological energies. From between the fittings of our ad-hoc craft, a gentle breeze blew.

"Victor, I think we've done it," Dewey said. I could muster no reply.

We looked at the controls: the return circuit was fully charged. A single tug and we would be home, with the warm glow of success… but not a scrap of evidence of it.

Dewey pressed his face against the glass, grinning with pleasure as that day's gentle sunlight warmed him.

He turned back to me, eyes gleaming. "Let's have a look!"

"That's what we're doing," I replied.

"Lets pop out—have a look about. Just for a moment."

Now, Eleanor, I know you believe yourself to have married a man who is—if not actually prudent—at least not entirely devoid of all common sense. A man, in other words, who would not sally forth into unknown conditions equipped with nothing but the clothing upon his back. I cannot describe how much it pains me to disabuse you of that happy illusion. All I can say in answer is that the view through the laboratory windows all morning had shown damp snow, coarsening eventually into heavy sleet rattling against the panes. The warm late spring day we beheld on the other side seemed an adventure of the most benign and inviting sort.

"Just for a moment," I agreed.

Dewey pulled the catch on the door and stepped out.

He stood in the grass, beckoning to me. "Well, come on then!"

I followed him through—and my foot fell on yielding grass, as I stepped from the chilly metallic Ontoscaphe into the full glory of a rural English spring. The lay of the land about us was, with careful scrutiny, familiar. The hills and valleys I beheld revealed that we were yet on the site of Tesla Hall, but now it was rolling green farmland, set about with little stands of trees, with a single carriage-path emerging from the woods to meander by our iron and glass monstrosity that crouched in a small hollow, a peculiar faint shimmer writhing above it like a strange desert mirage.

Dewey was lying in the grass now, hands behind his head, a perfect picture of contentment. "We have done it, Victor," he said dreamily, "our names shall be entered on the rolls of scientific fame alongside Newton, Faraday, Tesla, and Pierce."

I snorted in mirth. "I rather suspect that any club that counts Miss Pierce as a member is one from which Daedalus will waste no time in resigning. At any rate, don't you think it's time we went back home?"

Dewey looked petulant. "We still haven't any proof of having been here," he objected.

"Feel free to pick up a rock, or perhaps a cow-flop if you like," I told him. "Though I don't promise that they will persuade the scientific community. For real proof, we'll need to return with rifles, specimen-boxes, and daguerreotype machines. It isn't safe to remain here long without equipment."

"I suppose you are correct, Victor," Dewey conceded, and made for the 'scaphe with a great show of reluctance.

"Whatever is that?" he said, indicating with his hands the faint penumbra that enclosed our craft.

I squinted at it a moment, then extended my hand, which passed through the field without sensation of any kind. I shook my head. "An after-effect of the transition, I should suppose," I ventured.

We climbed inside and closed the hatch.

The machine was still humming and crackling happily, its massive battery well charged. I looked the dials over once more and pulled the return lever.

There was a brilliant flash of light and a report as if a charge of camera powder had gone off within the Ontoscaphe, and then all the dials sunk to zero.

Cursing, I crawled out of the cockpit once more, tugged the back panel open, and surveyed the instrumentation within. I took a long look in silence.

The largest of the thermionic valves in the circuitry appeared to have a crack running along its length.

Once it was unscrewed and held up in the light, it was unmistakably quite ruined.

"I shall have words with Hilgram and Sons about this," I said angrily. "That valve was nearly two pounds, and took three weeks to deliver; and here it has blown out after a single use! This is unforgivably shoddy workmanship."

"D'you think they have a Hilgram and Sons in this world, then?" Dewey asked.

"I shall have words with them when we return to our own world. In the meantime, I can only hope that they have such a thing as a thermionic valve here at all."

We looked about, the idyllic countryside about us transformed now from a refuge to a prison—a prison the size of the entire world. "What if the natives here are hostile?" Dewey said.

"Well, they—" I tried to say.

"What if they're cannibals?" He drew a great gulping breath. "What if they're hostile cannibals? What shall we do then?"

A faint smell of ozone provoked me to alarm. "Calm, Dewey," I said, with as soothing a tone as I could muster. "You must remain calm."

As we stood, trying to imagine what sort of inhabitants this place might have, a clattering noise, such as might be made by an exceptionally heavy carriage, became audible in the distance.

"The cannibals! They are coming for us!" Dewey cried in alarm, and reverted to his original form with a flash of blue light and a whiff of ozone. For months, it had seemed that he had gained an impressive degree of control over his tendency to transform in times of stress, but apparently the exceptional circumstances had overcome his resistance. Siphon-first, he nosed his way out of his collapsed clothes and took to the sky in a panic, leaving behind a drift of pinfeathers. For a moment, clam duck was silhouetted against azure sky, and then he had disappeared behind the treeline.

Hastily, I kicked his clothing into an unobtrusive pile, not wanting to have to explain their provenance to any interlopers. Even as I did so, a most extraordinary sight appeared between the trees. First two men, uniformed in brown livery, with pistol-belts, strode into view, calling out in alternation:

"Make way! Make way for the Erotofluidic Terminando!"

Then, with a clanking and clattering, came a massive device not unlike a carriage, but drawn by no visible steeds. Thinking it might be some sort of trackless locomotive vehicle, I looked about for an engine, but though it bore a large enclosed chamber in front, it generated no exhaust, and precious little noise, save for the whirring and clanking of its gears and a faint, almost musical sound akin to bird call. Where one might expect to see a driver—were it an ordinary coach—sat mounted a tall woman of aristocratic bearing, in a brown travelling dress akin in hue to the garb of her men, operating a bewildering array of knobs and levers of opaque function.

"Hold!" called the woman, who apparently was piloting the carriage, and she pulled a lever that brought her conveyance to a stop. The clanking ended at once, but the quieter, more musical noise continued unabated. The men stood at attention while their mistress stepped down unaided. A fourth member of the party, a colourless little fellow in pince-nez, in a uniform matching those of the others, emerged from within the conveyance and fussed with the metal cover.

"You there," the woman called to me. I had positioned myself to conceal as much of the Ontoscaphe as I could with my body. I was not taken with this person's abrupt manner of addressing me, but it was certainly not the moment to object aloud.

"Yes, madam, how may I be of service?" I said, hoping to inculcate courtesy by example if not by instruction."

"Is this the road to —————shire?"

Heedlessly, I replied: "If neither it nor the town has moved, it is."

She smiled thinly. "Ah, a humorist. Thank you very much, sir, for your exceptionally conservative reply." She gazed appraisingly at me for a moment.

"Have you served yet?" she asked me at last.

"I, er... I'm not quite certain what you mean," I confessed at last.

"Given service. To the crown."

"I... do my best," I ventured at last. "I do try to pay my income tax promptly."

Her smile this time had perhaps a hint of real warmth in it. "A wit indeed," she said. "And when was your last Terminando?"

The term was not entirely unfamiliar to me. *Audiendo et terminando* was the rather quaint phrase sometimes used to refer to the Assize. Had she taken me somehow for some sort of rustic barrister? "It's been... goodness... quite a while," I improvised lamely.

"Well then," she said. "I expect to see you at this afternoon's proceedings in —————shire. What is that unusual device behind you?"

"This old thing?" I said, affecting a casual air. "It's a... er... a threshing machine. Of my own invention."

She craned her neck to see better, as I held in place, attempting to block her view without appearing to do so. "A threshing machine," she said. "Does it work?"

"No, madam, it does not. No doubt my idea was unsound. But I must persist, until I have established that to my own certainty." An idea struck me—hazardous, but irresistible. "You do not happen to have such a thing about you as a spare thermionic valve, do you?" I asked, affecting a casual air.

Now, for the first time, she laughed, her even white teeth gleaming in the sunlight. "A thermionic valve! For a threshing machine!"

"It is a novel design," I conceded.

"The components of the ipsekinetron are not mine to distribute, I am afraid. I am merely a civil servant, and the *Albion* belongs not to myself, but to the crown."

My response mixed frustration with relief. This ontosphere apparently possessed technology sufficient to allow us to repair our damaged transport. Now it was merely a matter of access.

I was, of course, biting my tongue with effort not to interrogate this woman about her own remarkable conveyance, but if such things were commonplace in this world, it would be far too suspicious a query.

At any rate, more data was shortly forthcoming. The woman looked around and saw that the man was still struggling to lift the covering on the front of their craft. She gestured impatiently to the two guards. "Davis, Porter: lend Hodgkins a hand," she said briskly.

"Yes, Arbitor," they answered, and went to assist their fellow.

At last the three men succeeded in raising the cover, revealing to my startled eyes a pair of women, entirely naked so far as I could see (tho' that was only from the waist up), save for thin metal bands like steel tiaras that encircled their heads. They were both of middle years and quite attractive. It was evident even from a distance that they were gleaming with perspiration and flushed with some strong emotion. The curious noise I had noted proved to be these women's vocalization, for they cried out rhythmically, bouncing back and forth under the influence of some process that was occurring out of my sight.

The apparent leader of the party stood before them with a canteen in her hands. She tipped it to the lips of each woman in turn. They drank greedily from it, rivulets of clear fluid running down their necks and bare torsos.

Then, handing the canteen back to her men, she spoke: "Bunny, Dimples, how is it with you?"

"Oh, Arbitor," said the one nearer me, a plump, dark-haired beauty with heavy bosoms that cried out to be stroked and jostled. "I should like very much to spend. Please?"

The arbitor smiled sweetly. "Why, certainly, Bunny. You have been of excellent service today, and you are well deserving of some reward."

She reached up onto the panel and turned a dial, whereat a faint buzzing sound was to be heard, but only for an instant, before it was drowned out by the moans of the woman who had spoken before, who now commenced to writhe and bounce in such a manner that I became convinced that she must be bound both hand and foot within the conveyance.

Scarce a minute had passed when Bunny stiffened, eyes squeezing shut and tendons standing out in her neck as she attained her climax.

The arbitor twisted the dial once more, and the buzzing subsided; then she tenderly stroked Bunny's forehead, pushing back a stray lock of hair.

Then she turned to the other imprisoned woman. "Dimples," she said, "is there anything that you require?"

"That I—?" Dimples sputtered in response. "I require that you release me at once, that you return to me my clothes, and that you escort me at once back to my husband, before the consequences to you become any more dire."

The smile upon the arbitor's face did not diminish one iota, but something about her eyes subtly altered, and I found that I did not envy the foolish woman who had thus menaced her.

"I am afraid that is impossible," she said. "Two years, eleven months, three weeks, and five days yet remain of your service to the Crown."

Dimples blanched at this, cowed by the daunting duration cited, the invocation of her sense of civic duty, and not least by the steel in the voice of the formidable bureaucrat before her.

"In that case," she said in a meeker tone, eyes downcast, "I, too, would like to be permitted to spend."

The clothed woman chuckled throatily. "I am afraid that too is out of the question, for two reasons, either of which would be sufficient. Would you care to hear them?"

Dimples muttered something inaudible.

"Primus: through no fault of your own, you are possessed of a refractory period considerably longer than that of Bunny here. Thus, the steady and safe operation of the ipsekinetron requires that you not achieve over-much satisfaction before we have concluded for the day."

That said, she reached down and cupped the woman's chin, bringing her face up so that their eyes met. "Secundus: I do so like making you suffer. Questions? Concerns?"

To this there was no reply save Dimples's faint sobs.

The arbitor turned to her companions, who had stood attentively

throughout the foregoing exchange. "Seeing as it is such an exceptionally fair day, and ————shire is so near, I think we shall give
the girls a little air for the final leg of our journey. Hodkgins, make it
so."

The smallest of the three men sprang into action, retrieving a bag
of tools from the front of the conveyance and proceeding first to fix
the metal hood so that it would reliably remain open, and then to
raise the stools upon which the two women rested.

They straddled devices not unlike bicycle seats, their wrists fastened behind somehow. The purpose of the vertical extensions that
flanked them became apparent a moment later, as the men, over-
coming half-hearted resistance, took the women's limbs and raised
and spread them quite indecently, fastening them to the extensions
just above the knee, so that their hips were pressed forward, and their
richly-furred mottes forced into prominence.

Those lovely orifices were thus revealed to be impaled on shafts
which emerged from the seats and appeared to be attached to intricate
machinery that extended within the device.

In the minutes that this procedure consumed, the arbitor stood to
one side, jotting notes in a tiny leather-bound memorandum book. As
her assistant concluded his labours and put away his tools, she slipped
the book into one pocket and smoothed her skirts.

"Oh, Arbitor," cried Bunny, "we are to go into town like this?"

"Yes indeed," said the arbitor.

"Mightn't... mightn't you cover us then? To be exposed thus is so
very shameful."

The arbitor smiled sweetly. "Indeed it is, my dear," she said,
mounting the carriage to sit at the controls, above and behind the two
bound women. "Very shameful, indeed." She pulled a lever, and a
faint squeaking sound was followed an instant later by the motion of
the gleaming shafts that penetrated the two women, raising cries of
pleasure and distress from each in turn. "And that shame," she continued, speaking louder now to be heard over the machinery and her
two charges' cries, "contributes most usefully to the amount of erotic-
ity that your sweet little body generates."

She turned and acknowledged me for the first time since the initial interview. I think I had not moved an inch, so transfixed was I by the events before me. "Good day, sir," she called merrily.

"And now: onward to ————shire!"

With which words, she pulled another two levers, and the ipsekinetron juddered to life, proceeding down the road, the bound women emitting an extra dismayed yelp at each bump it passed over. Within a minute it had passed from sight between the trees, and in another two had faded into inaudibility.

I stood watching this bizarre procession disappear, lost in thought.

Dewey dropped out of the air beside me, returning to human form in time to make a somewhat graceless running landing. "I may have somewhat overreacted," he said sheepishly.

"No harm done," I assured him. "But get out of sight of the road. You are not currently fit for general consumption."

He looked quizzical for a moment, so I gestured to his naked form. "Oh, that," he said irritably. "You humans are so terribly fussy about this clothing business. It is sometimes rather tiresome, I must say."

"I shall have a stern word with the steering committee about it," I promised him dryly. "In the meantime, do please hasten to dress yourself. We need to follow that... conveyance."

"But the Ontoscaphe..." he objected, even while he struggled into his small-clothes.

"...does us no good at all without a fresh thermionic valve," I reminded him. "Do you want to stay here and guard it? For howsoever long it takes me to obtain one?"

"Alone?" he said, with a worried glance.

"As I thought. Come along, then."

Once more, as we set out, I looked back over my shoulder at our hoped means of escape. The afternoon light caught its gleaming brass sides so that the shimmer about it seemed almost to have strengthened since it had first caught our attention.

Chapter 2: The Arbitor

Fortunately, down in the village, we mingled well enough with the populace at large. The cut of their clothing was faintly quaint to my own eyes, and we drew a couple of quizzical glances—attributable as much, I suspect, to our being unfamiliar faces in so bucolic a locale as to any peculiarity of our appearance—but by and large we passed all but unnoticed as we made our way to the town square.

In time we found ourselves in the midst of a curious sort of jostling throng. It became clear that those in the rear were eagerly pushing forward, keen for a view of whatever proceedings lay ahead, whereas those at the front were drawing back with even greater ardour. The voices of the *Albion*'s two guards cut through the crowd's murmur, announcing the arrival of the Erotofluidic Terminando.

As we approached the front of the gathering, the strange bulk of the ipsekinetron came into view, the two women who powered it still writhing at its front, animate twin figureheads of unspeakable lewdness. Before our eyes it rolled to a stop, tho' the shafts penetrating the two women's cunnies continued their relentless thrusting. Nearer the device, the mechanisms of Vital Fluid collection and conduction were unmistakable, however unfamiliar the design. As surely as a junk or a dhow was a sailing-ship, this was a conveyance powered—however improbably—by Vital Fluids.

The arbitor's eyes swept the crowd appraisingly, and I felt a wave of unreasoning fear as they passed over myself, as if she would somehow divine our alien origins merely by looking into my eyes.

Davis and Porter were not idle, opening the door of the ipsekinetron and bringing down armloads of tarpaulin-shrouded equipment which they proceeded to reveal and assemble. I was fascinated with these unfamiliar devices, the elusive purpose of which tantalized my brain. Dewey's attention, however, was elsewhere. Taking my arm in an almost painful grasp, he pointed within the ipsekinetron, where its exposed motor whirred and hummed, holding in reserve the energies that provided its locomotion. And there—within its depths!—three massive thermionic valves hummed and glowed faintly, modulating the energies that passed through them.

I felt my heart quicken within my bosom. This was our means of return. I had been absent from my own ontological field a scant few hours, yet I was acutely aware of the terrible gulf that separated me from you, my precious beloved. Each hour in this strange and perverse world was an hour of absence from you and an hour of your uncertainty as to my own fate.

I belabour this point because theft was immediately in the front of my mind. Could I trust this strange, cruel woman with the secrets of our technology, our origin? No, too much was at stake! Dewey and I agreed: we would wait and see what opportunities might arise as events developed.

The necessary equipment unloaded, the arbitor brought the ipsekinetron to life, squeezing it into a narrow alleyway to make room around the array that Davis and Porter were assembling.

As the arbitor made her way back into the town square, the churn in the front rows became more pronounced as she reached the centre and looked coolly about. Curious though I was about this peculiar ritual, the prospect of those thermionic valves drew me yet more strongly, and Dewey and I struggled through the press of bodies towards the ipsekinetron and its priceless cargo. And good fortune it was, too. The arbitor was surveying the crowd with scientific interest. An electric charge seemed to follow her gaze, stirring its subjects to heightened agitation as it swept across them.

She pointed in our general direction. "That fellow there in the blue waistcoat." At once the young man in question was seized by half-a-dozen hands. "The very same," she affirmed, and he was fairly thrown forward, stumbling to remain on his feet. The colour was rising rapidly in his cheeks as he regained his feet and found the arbitor approaching him. She spoke quietly to him, and he fished within his shirt to draw out a little steel tag on a chain, which she scrutinized, then nodded. He was licking his lips rapidly. The arbitor pointed and spoke quietly, and the young man went and stood beside the bank of machinery, hands clasped uneasily in front of himself.

She turned to Hodgkins, who was seated before a broad bank of metres and dials. "Is all in readiness?" she said.

"Yes, Arbitor," he replied.

"Then let us begin."

She turned to the young man whom she had plucked first from the crowd. "James," she said, "I am going to be administering some tests to you now. Some of them will be pleasant for you. Some of them will be painful. Many of them are likely to be both." There was a ripple of laughter from the throng at this. "If you do not comply with my orders promptly, you will suffer a good deal more than you might otherwise. Now, undress."

James hesitated, then opened his mouth to speak.

"Yes, here, yes, now," she interrupted him impatiently. "Yes, in the town square in front of your friends, your sweethearts, and your employers." From the table, she lifted a gleaming brass rod, like a riding crop in size but forked at the end.

At the sight of it, the young man fairly sprang into action, unfastening his clothes with a haste that threatened to send the buttons flying across the square. Inside of two minutes, he was in a perfect state of nature; his slender manhood, alert to peculiar goings-on, standing out somewhat, his cheeks by now in a high flush, his arms crossed uncomfortably across his near-hairless chest.

"Good," the arbitor said. "Now put this on." She handed him the metal band that was so unmistakably a Vital Energies collector, and was attached by cables to the bank of equipment that the colourless man maintained.

"One," called Hodgkins, "Two... holding at two point four, Arbitor."

She stepped up to the naked man. "Clasp your hands behind your head," she told him.

When he complied, she traced the fingers on one hand down his bare chest, his flesh rippling visibly under her light touch. She paused, just below his navel, and his cock seemed to reach towards her hand like a plant straining towards sunlight, rising with each pulse of his heartbeat to draw nearer her palm.

"Wicked lad," she purred, and closed her slender hand about the shaft. A small noise came from between his pursed lips. "You are being so frustratingly obedient, I am presented with no excuse to employ the Motivator on you. I shall find one, you know. And I cannot wait to hear how you howl and sob when I do. Still, you may manage to delay the inevitable for some time."

As she spoke, she was lightly caressing the shaft and head of James's engorged member with her fingertips. It was now entirely rigid, the broad head crimson and shining. The muscles of his thighs were visibly straining to resist the urge to move his hips as she pleasured him.

"There are two ways to accomplish that. One is to be scrupulously obedient to my orders. That you are so far accomplishing, though it shall soon become much more difficult. The second," she tightened her grip upon his cock here, and another small noise escaped him, "is to avoid becoming excited by the tests we administer. If I subject you to cruelty, exposure, and humiliation, and you remain unmoved, you will be a free man until the next Terminando. If, on the other hand, you become sufficiently excited, your service to the crown begins this very day, and you will be entirely at my mercy for years to come."

"Which do you choose, James?" She released his member and began lightly smacking his cock, open-handed, making it bob wildly first to one side, then the other. "To return to your life, your village, your profession? Or to subject yourself to the Ministry, and to its cruel and lustful agents?"

James's distress was manifest upon his face, and he was whimpering piteously at each blow to his engorged organ, but, recognizing a rhetorical question when presented with one, he kept his quiet beyond those involuntary noises.

"Look about you, James," the arbitor coaxed, again taking his pego in her hand. "Look about you at your friends, your neighbours. If we haul you off tonight, naked and shackled, to employ you as a single human cog in the terrible machine of the Erotofluidic Age, each of them will know that your degradation was your own doing, that you are too wicked, too filthy to be able to avoi—"

James shuddered, and a drop of translucent fluid ran from the head of his cock down over her knuckles. In a sudden blur of motion, the arbitor had moved to the side, retaining her grip upon his pulsing penis, so that the first spurt of semen narrowly missed her, spattering instead on the cobblestones of the square.

She milked two more considerable gouts from James before he slumped into a posture of defeat. "Hodgkins?" she called.

"Four point seven," came the reply.

She clicked her tongue. "I worked much too rapidly. I am certain that this young man has a six in him."

"If you say so, Arbitor."

"At any rate, four-and-a-half is quite sufficient for our needs. Welcome to compulsory service, James. I am certain you have made the correct choice."

Davis escorted the unfortunate youth off while Porter gathered up his clothes. At this lull in the action, the spell that had fallen over the audience, Dewey and myself included, lifted momentarily.

"The valves," Dewey said to me.

"Not now," I answered. "We need to wait until they are all distracted again."

In little enough time, James had been settled somewhere out of the way, and the arbitor had scanned the crowd once more, selecting a woman who appeared to be a prosperous young housewife, presumably in town for her weekly shopping. I tore my eyes away from the progressive revelation of her ample figure to the task before us.

Our approach to the ipsekinetron from the back side went undetected as the two guards, busily craning their necks for glimpses of the proceedings at the centre, entirely neglected us. Bunny and Dimples regarded us with wide, anxious eyes, but whatever noises they made behind their gags were lost in the crowd's shouts and laughter.

It was the work of but a moment to slip within the carriage. A bright spark and a momentary popping noise had me jumping with alarm when I extracted one of the thermionic valves, but the disturbance was still insufficient to attract the attention of Davis and Porter.

"D'you suppose they have spares about?" asked Dewey.

"Almost certainly," I said, looking about at the mounded crates of equipment. "I rather fear they may be after us in short order."

"I have a plan," Dewey said, and he sprang out of the carriage.

I followed him to find that he was murmuring softly in Dimples's ear. One of his hands brushed against the lady's bare thigh, which twitched at the contact. "Dewey!" I whispered furiously. "Is this really the time——?"

He shushed me with an impatient gesture of his left hand, while his right slid down the bound woman's limb, until he reached the furred mound where she was speared on the metal shaft. She whimpered as his fingers traced the mouth of her vulva.

Torn between impatience and fascination, I watched as Dewey, finding Dimples to be already in an advanced state of arousal, wasted no time in pressing his fingers to her engorged clitoris while the knuckles of his other hand brushed over one dark, crinkled nipple. The woman let out a long, loud groan.

"Hush," Dewey urged her. "You wouldn't want to upstage the arbitor's performance, would you? I don't think she would take kindly to that." His fingers stopped rotating on Dimples's genitals, and her eyes opened wide in dismay. She desperately attempted to rub herself against his teasing hand but soon realized that he was awaiting a response. She shook her head in furious negation.

"Good," Dewey said, and resumed, this time eliciting a drawn-out shudder, but no sound but the forceful intake of breath. "You're going to spend for me, aren't you, Dimples, and you're going to do it very quietly."

She nodded vigourously at this, clearly eager to please him by any means she could. She flushed darker with each passing moment, her breath coming in little shuddering pants as her toes, elevated above her head by the position in which she was bound, flexed and extended in rapid spasms.

Dewey gripped her nipple between thumb and forefinger and tugged at it firmly; as her body froze in place, his motions upon her clitoris slowed a bit, serving only to lengthen and intensify her climax. With impressive self-restraint, only the least whimper passed her lips before she slumped into relaxation in her bonds.

Gently, Dewey caressed her hair for a moment. "You have done very well, Dimples. Thank you."

Then he turned to me. "Best we make haste," he said, then walked off, sucking contentedly at his fingers.

It was our extraordinary ill fortune that the second subject's Terminando was just concluding as we tried to shove our way out of the town square. Apparently the woman had failed to make the grade, as she was resuming her clothes with an expression that appeared to my eye to mingle relief with disappointment, all overlaid on the lingering shame and erotic excitement of her late adventure.

I glanced towards the centre of the square, just in time for my eyes to meet those of the arbitor. "Ah, our inventor!" she called out. "Won't you come forward, sir!" But before that sentence could leave her lips, I was turned in a panic, attempting to make a run for it, the precious valve tight in my grasp.

The crowd surged about me, though, pressing me towards the square, a seething mass of gleeful schadenfreude.

Her expression faded as the crowd shoved me forward. "What is that you have in your hand?" she said sharply.

Too late, I attempted to conceal the thermionic valve, nearly as big as my head, behind my back. A moment later, it was wrenched out of my grip and held aloft by the grinning Davis.

The arbitor's nostrils flared as she strode towards us briskly. I braced myself for her fury, but instead she halted, her face inches from Davis's. "You let this scoundrel board the *Albion* and pluck valuable components out of its engine?" she demanded.

Davis, who had looked so self-satisfied a moment before, blanched at this. "I, er, er.... We have it back now, Arbitor," he said.

"Well, isn't that fortunate for you."

Davis wisely said nothing.

She turned to me. "I really ought to turn you over to the constabulary," she said in an almost conversational tone. "It is quite what you deserve. However, I am sadly notorious for the sweetness and malleability of my nature."

She paused, as if expecting me to argue. I did not.

"The Ministry is empowered to conscript lawbreakers, who have not previously had their terms of service, summarily, and at its own discretion. I am quite certain that so spirited a fellow as yourself will have an exemplary fluidic index, and will be a valuable addition to my collection. No need to test you now, though, since you are not walking free, no matter the outcome."

She turned to Davis once more. "Hold onto our friend here for the time being. And do kindly try not to lose him."

Porter returned the valve to the ipsekinetron while Davis led me—none too gently—over to the erotometer. His scowl suggested that he had decided to blame me for his current disfavour with his employer.

From that vantage, I scanned the crowd for Dewey's face. I didn't have to search long, as the great ninny was waving anxiously at me. I shook my head furiously, trying to get him to make himself less conspicuous. But I was too late. He had caught not just my attention, but the arbitor's as well.

For a moment she was appeared taken aback by his gesticulations, then she laughed. "A volunteer! How refreshing!" she said. "Very well, sir, step forward and be tested."

Dewey's mouth fell open in alarm, but the crowd pushed him forward, and in a moment he stood in the middle of the square with me.

I felt some small concern as to Dewey's mental state. When I glanced at him, his eyes were shut tightly. He was repeatedly mouthing something that I soon realized was "Stay calm; don't panic." I wondered anxiously, even if Dewey managed to forestall the transformation that was in danger of overtaking him, how long it would take for our captors to notice the flickering blue penumbra that was beginning to surround him.

"Prepare him," the arbitor ordered, and Dewey was hauled along towards the testing apparatus.

"Stay calm," he yelped, "don't panic!"

As Dewey was hauled over to the strangely wrought collection stand, the arbitor remained behind me. She leaned down, and I felt her hot breath against my ear. "We are performing the rest of the Terminando first, because I am a firm believer in delayed gratification," she said very quietly, "but I am very much looking forward to seeing what you are capable of. Beyond deceit, larceny, and vandalism, that is."

Dewey's waistcoat and small-clothes were roughly pulled open, not without the loss of several buttons. Throughout the proceedings, Dewey continued to mutter to himself, struggling to forestall the transformation which panic could induce in him.

"Hodgkins, fire up the testing apparatus," the arbitor said. "Porter, remove the rest of his clothes. Davis, make yourself useful and take down the information of our new guest. I shall see whether our latest subject makes a better compulsory than he does a conversationalist."

The men sprang to obey their orders. I watched Davis and Porter as the one roughly undressed my friend, who was too dazed to offer either resistance or aid, while the other gathered up pen, ink, and blotting paper.

Rather than attempt to fabricate a tale, I merely toned down the truth. I was assistant to Daedalus Tesla, I told them, a local gentleman of means, serving as secretary and amanuensis, and assisting him at his scientific research. (I had a whole soliloquy of dreary fabrications on the topic of agricultural machinery prepared if the nature of that research was inquired into. It was not.)

Had the arbitor been involved in my interrogation, I am certain that there would have been a number of probing questions as to my master's involvement in our larcenous acts, but Davis, bureaucrat to the core, omitted those queries for which there was no space available on his pre-printed form.

I was distracted from this conversation by an arresting buzzing, rattling noise. I looked around to find that Dewey was quite nude, eyes still shut, still muttering to himself, in counterpoint to the arbitor's own urgent, quiet words, unrecognisable at this distance. His rigid cock was in her hand, and she was tugging rhythmically at one of his nipples, hard enough to elicit a squeak with each squeeze.

The rattling noise came from the testing apparatus. The previously colourless Hodgkins looked quite agitated now, a sheen of sweat across his forehead; his gaze was firmly on the dials before him.

"Arbi—" he began.

"Silence!" she barked, then resumed her hushed coaxing.

The blue radiance that had surrounded Dewey had intensified, now running up the length of the cable that ran from his head to the apparatus.

"I wouldn't do that if I were you," I called out.

Davis ignored my outburst, but appeared transfixed by the shuddering, glowing equipment. "What sort of man could overload a Ministry erotometer?" he said, more to himself than me.

The signs were all too familiar. "Duck!" I exclaimed.

Davis looked back at me, and his brow furrowed. The erotometer by now was drifting across the tabletop, propelled by its violent vibrations.

"Get down!" I insisted.

When he still failed to take my advice, I despaired of communicating with this astoundingly obtuse man, and flung myself to the floor. An instant later, there was a series of sharp reports, followed by screams of alarm and pain as shards of glass embedded themselves in the exposed flesh of experimenters and spectators alike.

I stood, and, just before billowing smoke enclosed him, I saw Dewey gesturing to me to flee. There was no time to hesitate—I broke into a sprint, followed, seconds later, by Davis, clearly anxious not to further incur the arbitor's displeasure.

The churning, panicked crowd had no attention to spare for me, and I made it through with reasonable dispatch, followed by angry shouts from the yeomen I shoved aside. Davis and I proved closely matched competitors as I ran, with no conscious destination, through largely deserted streets; only a few old farmers and their wives had failed to heed the summons to the Terminando, the massive guardsman ever close at my heels.

It was only when I saw the massive black column of smoke from a locomotive that I fully realized where I had been heading—the train station. It was my great good fortune that its location was unchanged from my own world.

Luck remained with me as I reached the platform: the train was already gaining steam. Rather than ducking in prematurely, I ran alongside as it accelerated, Davis still only yards behind me. He called to the conductors to stop me, but the roar of the engine drowned him out. At the last possible instant, I sprang in the door, knocking an oblivious conductor to the floor beneath me. Davis's final burst of desperate speed was a valiant effort, but I was clear.

I picked myself up off the unfortunate functionary, then helped him to his feet. Still scarlet-faced, dripping with perspiration, and gasping for breath, I reached into my pocket to pay for a ticket. For a moment, I was seized by fear—would my banknotes pass muster here?—but the conductor was too occupied glowering at me for my breach of locomotive etiquette to spare much scrutiny or comment for my currency, and he directed me to the nearest unoccupied compartment with bad grace but no delays.

I surveyed my situation: a few pounds in my pocket; a broken Ontoscaphe awaiting discovery in an open field my only hope of eventual return home; my companion lost; my trousers none the better for my tumble into the train car. It was not an easy row to hoe, as they say in the agricultural-implement field.

Chapter 3: The Viola

I found myself obscurely comforted by the familiar sights, sounds, and smells of a coal-fired steam locomotive. I was not alone for long—the next station was rather full, and eventually a man entered, begging my pardon for the intrusion, and sat across from me by the window. As he figures considerably in the narrative to come, I shall describe him in some detail now, though I made little enough note at the time. He reminded me a bit of Daedalus, with his dark complexion, modest stature, and an air of self-confidence to the point of arrogance. He was broader of build, though, with a face that might be termed cherubic were it less serious, and a faintly pugnacious swagger in place of Daedalus's intellectual abstraction.

I knew that, for the time being, the less unnecessary interaction I engaged in with the natives of this ontosphere, the better. Who could say what chance remark would display incongruous ignorance (or knowledge), branding me as something other than I appeared? Thus, I responded to this newcomer with the vaguest and briefest possible greeting. He rested a folded newspaper on the seat at his side and fixed his attention on the rolling hills outside. My eyes were drawn to that newspaper. What information might it reveal to me about the state of the world in which I found myself trapped?

I was plunging towards the terrible Colossus of London, impoverished and friendless, having abandoned my only companion to slavery and left my only means of escape unguarded in an open field. Remorse, apprehension, and resolve all did battle within my breast.

"My dear fellow," the man across from me said, in a rather husky tenor, "if you want this newspaper so very much, you are quite welcome to it! I ask only that you leave the cross-word puzzle undone. I do so enjoy those."

Apparently my look of apprehension and longing had been interpreted as being directed at this man's newspaper. Well, no need to look a gift-horse in the mouth. I gratefully accepted the proffered document, and scanned the headlines:

THOPTER CROSSES CHANNEL; DAVIDSON, FITZHUGH GREETED BY CHEERING CROWDS IN NORMANDY

RAMSEY STEATED IN COMMONS; LIBERAL MP THIRD VIOLA

MofEF CALLS FOR 20% BUDGET INCREASE; DICKSINSON CALLS SAFETY, COMFORT OF COMPULSORIES 'NATIONAL DUTY'

The articles that followed were similarly gnomic, illuminating their subjects only in flashes. The thopter was some sort of flying-machine, it seemed. MofEF turned out to be the Minister of Erotofluidics. The second article's dark hints about the growing power and legitimacy of the violas remained, however, opaque. The tone of the article suggested that they combined all the least-endearing qualities of Freemasons, Socialists, and malaria, but this was implied rather than ever stated.

"Quite an accomplishment, eh?" said the man across from me.

I started out of my studies and looked at him.

"The channel crossing," he clarified.

I nodded agreeably. "Why, how long has it been since they were saying man would never fly?"

Somewhat disappointingly, he took the question as rhetorical, and merely nodded.

"You'll notice," he said a moment later, cocking one eyebrow, "that they never mention that FitzHugh is another viola. Don't want to 'taint' such an accomplishment for the Empire, no doubt."

"The selective attention of the press is apparently a universal constant," I ventured.

He chuckled heartily at this. "Just so, just so!" Then he extended one hand. "Alex Weaver," he said.

I took it. "Victor Dalrymple."

"A great pleasure," he said warmly. He held the grip a moment longer, his eyes fixed on mine, and something in the tenor between us shifted, not unpleasantly.

"Where are you bound?" he inquired.

"London. There is some specialized scientific apparatus I need, and it seems the most likely place to start my search."

He blinked several times at this, then lowered his head. "You may have some time to kill, then."

I licked my lips. Darling Eleanor, you know better than any that my favour runs predominantly to your own sex. And yet the prospect of a dalliance with this fellow was singularly appealing to me at that moment. A distraction from the weight of my troubles seemed just the thing at that moment, and Mr. Weaver was an exceptionally personable individual. I shifted my position, better to accommodate the swelling of my pego, and Weaver's eyes flickered downward appraisingly.

"I know a few ways to make the landscape pass a bit quicker, if you fancy a bit of risk," Weaver offered.

"My luck with train compartments has been passable in the past," I said.

I was about to rise and go over to him when he beat me to the punch, gracefully sinking to the floor between my knees, his eyes fixed on mine in a most arresting fashion. He opened my flies with startlingly deft fingers, and extracted my rapidly hardening affair.

He pressed his hands against the tops of my thighs, darting for the head of my cock, then pausing for a moment to draw out the pleasure of anticipation for both of us. Then the heat and compression of his mouth was upon me, and I stifled a groan at the exquisite sensation.

In some areas of endeavour, there is but a single perfect way to perform them; and all approaches are excellent exactly insofar as they approximate it. In others, there are as many forms of excellence as there are excellent practitioners, each adept perfecting his own craft, distinct from any other before or since. Such a realm, I believe, is cock-sucking, and just as there has never been a fellatrix so perfectly Eleanor Dalrymple-y as yourself, so the heights of Alexander Weaverdom I experienced that afternoon were beyond any I had ever before known.

He devoured me with an urgency befitting our risky circumstances, yet I venture that he would likely have displayed a similar impatience even in perfect seclusion. He groaned approvingly when I rested my hand on his head, and, by increments, I soon found myself pulling him down onto my rigid affair, heedless of the pomade that now coated my hands, egged on by his muffled sounds of encouragement, even as his eyes watered and his face flushed.

At last, he pushed back against my hands and then, after a few heaving gasps, took my shaft in his hand and squeezed. "What a marvellous cock you have, Dalrymple," he murmured to me, though I blush to quote it. "How I long to taste your hot spunk."

I gasped at that confession, and my cock surged in his hand.

"Say that again, and you shall," I admitted to him.

He nodded, stroking my cock. "I want you to spend in my mouth, Dalrymple. I want to take your sperm in my—"

Some sixth sense alerted him to the imminence of my climax, and he sealed his lips over the head of my member just as I bit back a long groan and ejaculated in several long surges.

I closed my eyes, overwhelmed by the sensation, and when I opened them again, he was seated across from me, taming his hair with one hand and dabbing at his lips with a handkerchief in the other. "Best put that rammer away, or the rest will be wanting some, too," he said, nodding to my still-exposed genitals.

"Just so," I said, and had only just fastened the last button when a train-butch suddenly thrust his head through the compartment's curtains. "Newspaper, si—" he began, then, seeing that I was already adequately supplied, began again: "Candy, cigars, roast nuts?"

"No, thank you," I said. My meagre funds left no room for indulgences. I inclined my head, however, towards my compartment-mate. The butch followed my motion and noticed him for the first time, swallowing hard and paling slightly. He opened his mouth, presumably to repeat his practised pitch, but no sound came out.

My new friend seemed neither surprised nor perturbed by this odd response, but smiled reassuringly. "I'll have a packet of nuts, if it is not too much trouble," he said.

He might have said "I'll have your spleen on a pointed stick" for all the pleasure the butch showed at the news.

"Soon, preferably."

The butch yelped and disappeared.

There was a moment's silence.

Then the butch was edging back into the car, quite the reverse of his original heedless rush. He extended the waxed-paper bag between two fingertips. The bag was taken, and silver flashed through the air in a sparkling arc. The boy had barely the presence of mind to fumblingly catch the tossed coin after it after it had bounced off of his sternum. "A shilling for your troubles," my seatmate said.

The boy stared at it, saucer-eyed. "Thank you," he mumbled.

Weaver cocked his head and raised an eyebrow.

"...sir." said the butch.

A second coin followed the first. "Excellent lad. Now be off, and God keep you."

The butch disappeared in an instant, and my seatmate took a nut, then offered the bag to me.

I gratefully took as many as seemed consistent with courtesy. "Did that boy know you?"

He chuckled. "Not personally," he said.

"You were very generous with him," I said.

"I do what I can to show that we violas aren't such terrible monsters."

"Monsters!" I exclaimed. "Why, if you are any sort of exemplar, I shall have to join them myself!"

My new friend positively threw back his head and howled with laughter. I chuckled wanly, concerned that I had somehow revealed my ignorance of this ontosphere's peculiarities. He leaned forward and companionably gripped me by the shoulder. "Unless you have discovered the secrets of ontological engineering, I am afraid that may prove difficult."

I gaped, but he was fortuitously occupied with wiping the tears of mirth from his eyes, and failed to notice my expression.

I was mulling how to further probe my new friend's knowledge of these matters when he ventured: "I say, not to pry, but do you know where you will be staying in London?"

"I do not!" I admitted. "How did you guess?"

He leaned forward. "Quite frankly, Dalrymple, you appear to be a man beset by troubles. Your trousers, fine though they are, have seen better days, your hair is a mess, and, most strikingly of all, you have apparently failed to note that you have boarded the northbound train to Manchester, not the southbound to London."

I used several words which I try not to deploy lightly, but which seemed entirely warranted by current circumstances.

"Further," he continued, "if I am any judge of such things (and I fancy that I am), you had not spent in several days, at least."

I pursed my lips. The bare rudiments of such a plan as I possessed were now in shambles. I doubted I could even afford a rail ticket to London, the shorter distance having consumed more than half of my funds.

Weaver cleared his throat. "My club does have spare rooms," he ventured. "Generally available for brothers in need of them, but a friend of the Brotherhood such as yourself would be welcome to stay for a short time."

I shook my head sadly. "You have already shown me considerable kindness, Weaver," I protested. "To take further charity from you—"

"Well, perhaps it needn't be charity," he interrupted. "Are you a man of trade?"

"Of a sort," I equivocated. "I have some skill in book-keeping...." Then I drew a deep breath and gambled. "And some little knowledge of... of ontological engineering."

Weaver raised his eyebrows. "Practical ontological engineering?"

"Extremely," I responded, with all the conviction I could muster.

"You are serious, aren't you," Weaver breathed.

"Entirely."

"Then, yes, I believe a barter could be very mutually beneficial."

The club in question was, Weaver revealed, the Fraternal Order of St. Joan.

"This is—pardon my asking—a papist organization?"

"Not at all," he reassured me. "It is, by and large, a perfectly ordinary gentleman's club."

"Good cigars, bad port, late-night rubbers, and uninformed political opinion?"

"I see you have some familiarity with the genre."

"The Daguerreotype Society is my preferred watering hole in London. Or, at least it was, back in—" I caught myself before saying more than I meant to. "—its heyday."

From the station, we caught a hansom-cab to the club, which turned out to be a rather imposing brick building with a neoclassical façade, dominated by Joan herself, twice life-sized, in marble, decked in a suit of plate mail, hair cropped scandalously short, and gazing out at the busy street with a sort of martial calm. We passed that unnerving sentry's scrutiny into a tiled receiving room, where Weaver had a brief consultation with a fresh-faced young man, then led me through a handsome common room with a large fireplace. A dozen or so brothers were taking their leisure, reading the newspaper or clustered about the billiard tables. As with many clubs, the members of the Order of St. Joan appeared to be rather a type. At first glance, I thought them rather a young group, but a second look showed a fair proportion of grey hairs among the assembled gentlemen; it was the smallish builds and clean-shaven faces of the Joanites that had misled me. Before I could make further study of the matter, we had reached a stairwell, which proved to lead up to a snug but well-appointed room on the first floor.

"It isn't much," he said as he led me in, "but—"

"Not a word of it!" I interrupted him. "You have been an enormous benefactor to me already. I do not know how I can thank you enough." I shut the door behind him, and it closed with a satisfying click. "But I do have a notion of how I can start."

I pressed him up against the shut door and kissed him, his mouth opening eagerly to me after a moment, his hands sliding under my jacket to embrace me. We enjoyed each other's mouths for a long moment before I pulled back and gasped for breath.

"Your generosity with me is an area where I am not in a position to even the score at the time. Your cock-sucking, however, is."

He drew breath between his teeth, and his hands slipped down to his trousers, where they began to unfasten the buttons.

"I'm going to suck your cock, Weaver," I announced. "You denied me the opportunity on the train, but you won't deny me now."

His expression changed. "My... cock," he said, in a curious tone.

"Yes," I persisted, and attempted to emulate his own thrilling knack for randy language: "I'm going to take your rigid pego in my mouth and suck on it until you spend."

When Weaver spoke, it was in a curious sort of flat voice. "You don't know what a viola is, do you?"

I swallowed hard, suddenly feeling very much on the spot. "Well... it's a sort of Whiggish... group," I ventured.

Weaver nodded slightly, and his hands reversed their prior process, re-fastening his trouser buttons. He disentangled himself from me and opened a cabinet on one side of the room, revealing a small but well-stocked bar. He poured two whiskies, and handed me one of them.

"Dalrymple, I am, as I have told you, a viola. That means that, although I am a gentleman, I have the body of a woman." He took a largish drink of his whiskey as I digested this information.

"Where?" I asked.

He snorted, followed by a brief but intense coughing fit. "Under my clothes, you great twit!" he gasped between coughs and gulps of breath.

"So you're really a—?"

With an effort, he composed himself. "I am really a gentleman," he said firmly, "though I was not born so."

I digested this intelligence. "So all the members of your club...?"

"Are the same in this regard."

"Fascinating!" I said, looking at my friend in a new light. He, in turn, gazed fixedly at his drink. I realized that he was apprehensive as to my reaction.

"I've never gamahuched a gentleman before," I allowed. "But, if you will permit me, I should very much like to essay it."

He grinned and rose to his feet. "I was so hoping you would say that."

One of his hands took the back of my neck, and when he spoke again, all his prior cockiness seemed restored. "It is rather a shame," he said quietly. "I am certain you are an excellent cock-sucker." The thumb of his other hand ran over my lips before pushing demandingly at my jaw. I opened compliantly and sucked at it.

He shuddered with pleasure, then reluctantly withdrew his hand. It dug beneath his waistcoat, then downward. The other tightened on the back of my neck as he groaned aloud at whatever was transpiring within his trousers.

A moment later, two shining fingers were pressed against my lower lip, and I was hungrily taking them into my mouth until I felt the close-trimmed nails against my soft palate. My tongue worked busily at their undersides, savouring the thick nectar of his excitement that coated them.

After a time, he replenished his supply, thrusting his hand within his trousers once more, his brow knitting as he penetrated himself; then pushing his fingers—three in number now—into my mouth to be cleaned.

Then he was unfastening his trousers while I watched, eager to have a look at the body beneath his clothes.

I was not disappointed. Broad hips had been skilfully de-emphasized by his well-tailored trousers. His mons was covered with dark hair, tightly curled, and, had my salivary glands not already been operating at full tilt, they would surely have woken to that appetizing sight.

Barred from further disrobement by his boots, he shuffled, a bit awkwardly, to the bed, and fell backward upon it. He brought his legs up and hooked his arms behind his knees. Thus displayed, the swollen lips of Weaver's cunny were pressed apart, revealing the glistening crimson orifice between. Nor was the dark knot of his bottom-hole a sight lost on my hungry eyes.

"Well, get over here, Dalrymple," Weaver called with mock irascibility. "I shan't lie here all day like this."

"Right away, sir!" I said at once, and were you to ask me whether it was said in mockery or sincere submission, I could not tell you with certainty. I sprang to the bedside, only to kneel and bow my head, praying at that most ancient and holy of temples. I ate the body of my benefactor, and drank his sacramental fluids, while he cried out his passion.

"Discretion, my dear fellow," I admonished him breathlessly, after a particularly piercing howl.

"Discretion be d—-ed!" he answered. "There's none but Brothers here, and if they object, it shall be only because they weren't invited to join the fun. If you are half the cock-sucker that you are a cunny-lapper, you must be the most well-liked man in all ————shire."

"You are too kind," I demurred, "I really—mmmf!"

Weaver had contrived somehow to extricate one arm from his tangled trousers, and he used it to shove my unresisting face back into his splayed cunt.

Lacking any objections to his implicit demand, I turned my attention to lapping at his engorged clitoris and pressed a finger into his vagina, finding it quite as wet and swollen as I had anticipated. I curled my finger upward, pressing the tip against the pad of resilient flesh I found there.

"That!" Weaver gasped. "That, that, that!"

I followed his advice, replicating the operation as precisely as I could.

Eventually, I decided to raise the stakes of our game, bringing a second finger to bear. His clitoris swelled palpably beneath my tongue, his hand gripping painfully at the back of my head.

"I—I—I spend!" he called out, then the soft pad against which my fingers had been pushing pressed back, nearly exiling my fingers from their warm, moist home. His whole body convulsed as he let out a hoarse cry, then slumped bonelessly to the bed, his trousered knees straddling my neck like a yoke.

I struggled out of this confinement and unlaced his boots while he babbled contentedly, eventually removing them, followed by his trousers.

I lifted his limp ankles and pressed them up to their former position. "Just take hold of these once more, there's a good fellow," I urged him.

"Just need to recover my..." he murmured before trailing off, but wrapped his arms 'bout his knees compliantly enough.

I kneeled once more, but lowered my attention, bringing my mouth to the orifice which he bore in common with more ordinary-issue gentlemen.

"Oh," Weaver sighed. "Oh, that's rather lovely."

I thrust my tongue tip, with gentle persistence, against that resilient little knot of muscle, already damp with the fluids that had dripped down during our prior connection. He cooed and sighed contentedly as I performed the devil's kiss, undulating his hips in a languid fashion.

Over time, his bottom-hole relaxed, allowing my tongue further penetration. I stood and hastily stripped off my own clothes, until I stood entirely naked. Weaver, heels resting now on the edge of the bed, cupped his swollen vulva with one hand. "Is this still you showing your gratitude?" he asked.

"No," I confessed, "this is me about to fuck you because I wish to."
"Tsk! Such selfishness."

All through this badinage, his eyes never left my cock, as I placed myself between his legs and pushed down my rigid member to slide along the groove of his pussy, making it shine with the accumulated fluids there. He squirmed appreciatively at the contact, but frowned when I bent my prick further down, so that it nosed eagerly against his opening. "Have a care, sir," he warned me. "You do not wish to do me an injury."

"I most certainly do not," I agreed, and lowered my cock-head still further, until it nudged up against his bottom-hole.

"There should be some French letters in the armoire..." he said hastily.

"Ah, but what is a gentlemen's club without buggery?" I said, easing my hips forward to press the purple head of my prick against his yielding little pucker.

"Well, do be careful with that great truncheon of yours," he said. (I report merely what I was told!) "I haven't had anything of that girth up my bottom-hole in weeks."

Agreeably, I slowed my motions still more, working the crown of my prick against his bottom in gentle, minuscule thrusts, increasing the force and depth by slow increments. Our eyes locked as the head breached that line of defence, and he let out a long, low groan. I held there for a long moment before pressing my advantage, pressing within another inch, then luxuriating in that limited penetration, thrusting shallowly. Weaver's hand was not idle on his cunt, slowly tugging at his clitoris in counterpoint to my thrusts.

At last, I was fully within him, my hips pressed against his bottom. "Dirty bugger," he growled.

"Filthy little catamite," I answered.

His hands clutched at my hips, holding me in place. Each pulsation in my excited cock caused him to suck breath through his teeth and drew an answering squeeze from his distended sphincter, so that we soon were feeding back to each other a series of exquisite sensations, even as I laboured to hold my hips in place and restrain the growing urge to thrust.

In time, he nodded slightly, and urged me with his hands to commence a slow motion within him.

Above the waist, he was still fully dressed, shirt-tails tucked up out of the way under his waistcoat, cravat understandably askew. Below the waist was the fascinating sight of his luscious cunny, the rapid oscillations of his hand on his clitoris revealing and concealing its intricate folds by turns, and below that the shaft of my pego disappearing between the pale cheeks of his bottom. The juxtaposition of masculine garb and feminine anatomy was a wonderfully piquant sight, and my eyes roamed restlessly from his flushed, handsome face to his stretched bottom-hole, keen not to miss a single fascinating detail.

He urged me on more vigourously with each passing moment, resting his ankles on my shoulders. His busy hand left his clitoris to press two, then three fingers within his cunt to the knuckle. We both groaned aloud as his bottom hole squeezed me with even greater compression, his fingers massaging my shaft through the thin membrane between the two orifices.

"Give it to me, Dalrymple," he urged me on, "spare not an ounce of your strength."

I was bent forward now, hands indenting the mattress as my bare belly rubbed against the fine wool of his waistcoat, shaking the bed with the violence of my thrusts. Our mouths sealed together, muffling our combined cries, my movements now rapid and undisciplined, his knuckles digging into my groin as he continued to frig his cunt. He cried out, his fingers clutching bruisingly at my flank, and gripped at my cock, that sensation driving me to join him in climax, until, spent, I collapsed onto him, my softening prick still lodged in his bottom.

"Whoreson bastard, I shan't sit comfortably for a week," he said happily.

"Longer, if I catch you 'tween now and then," I promised.

Chapter 4: The Brotherhood

After we had regained our clothing and straightened our cravats, Weaver led me down to the club's bar, which was just starting to fill up with evening custom. We sat on high leather stools, and the barkeep—another young man in livery—brought us sherries.

"The staff here are violas too?" I asked him.

"Newbies," he said.

The term was unfamiliar to me, and I said as much.

Weaver assumed a pedantic expression. "The Brotherhood was founded, a little less than a century ago, by four wealthy violas, well before that term had come into common use. Francis Newberton was the first applicant to join subsequent to that time. He pledged himself to service to the founding brothers, in whatever capacity they might desire, until such time as they saw fit to admit him to their circle. Initiates are generally referred to as Newbertons in his honour. After the manner of such terms, it is oft shortened to Newbs or Newbies."

"Free labour! Very wise."

"Well, yes. And a degree of privacy that more ordinary hired help cannot offer."

I nodded, then changed the subject. "You had a problem in ontology to put to me."

"In ontological engineering," Weaver corrected me, "if such a thing is indeed possible. The thing is like this: For myself, I am pleased with the anatomy I have been bestowed by nature—"

"As am I."

"Hush! I am pleased, as I was saying, but many of my brothers feel a tension between their forms and their spirits."

"Cartesians, eh?"

"Hush, I say! It is a tension that they aspire to reconcile." He paused significantly.

"You mean—?"

"Yes. They tire of having to remove their godemiches to use the privy."

"But it's not just about pricks. They want the full package."

"You are a quick study."

"I wonder if they have any notion what an abominable nuisance shaving is."

"Spoken like a gentleman who has never experienced menses."

"You have read me aright in that regard, I confess. An hour ago, I had no idea another sort of gentleman existed."

"So, such an operation. Is it possible?"

"I have seen greater deeds by far done through ontological power...."

"But?"

"It is a strange and unpredictable force, still only dimly understood. Such a procedure would run a considerable risk of... of unexpected consequences."

"There are those among the Joanites who would risk all for this. If you can offer them any hope at all, they will seize it. We have ample laboratory space here at the club; what implements we do not have, we can obtain; funds should be little object for an endeavour of this gravity."

"Excellent. I have many more questions for you, and more than a few answers. I know you are acutely curious as to my own circumstances, but I beg your forbearance for a few days yet. I have strange things to tell, and I wish to show you that I am no madman before I do so."

"I confess, my curiosity, which was indeed formidable, is only made more piquant by your demurral. But I shall wait, with as much patience as I can bring to bear."

"Good man. Now let me have a look at these laboratory facilities in which you take such pride."

∽

The facilities proved to be quite as lavish as Weaver had promised, tho' with a dilettante's haphazardness. Chemical retorts were half-buried behind a massive and intricate clockwork device that Weaver told me was a "Lovelace engine." (He said it did sums, but I could not tell if he spoke in jest.) In one corner rested a handsome replica of Merry-weather's Tempest Prognosticator, several of its leeches now gone to whatever reward awaits their kind. A great wooden crate of thermionic valves of every size and description made me sigh melancholically. Twenty-four hours ago, a single one of these would have been the solution to all our troubles. Now Dewey was in bondage to that daemonic arbitor, the Ontoscaphe doubtless seized by the Ministry of Erotofluidics—the troubles before us seemed only to multiply with each passing moment.

My first night in that world was largely a sleepless one. Already, I missed you terribly, my darling. My snug little bed seemed a bare prison of solitary confinement without my Eleanor on the pillow beside me. How I craved your gentle touch, your sweet voice. Visions of the agony of uncertainty I was putting you through pursued me through the night. When I succeeded in pushing that from my mind, the thought of Dewey subjugated to the cruel arbitor rose before me in its place.

In the morning, Weaver let me know that he had arranged a meeting with the President of the Order, to allow me to put my case to him.

President Purslaine proved to be an exceedingly diminutive man with very short hair the colour of steel and a gaze reminiscent of the same alloy. He rose from his massive mahogany desk when I entered his office and shook my hand very firmly before gesturing me to a very comfortable leather chair and offering me a cigar.

We lit up in silence, and then he peered appraisingly at me though a cloud of thick blue smoke. "Weaver speaks highly of you, Mr. Dalrymple," he said at last.

"I am delighted to hear it," I said cautiously.

When I failed to say more, he prompted me: "I understand you have a proposition to put to the Brotherhood."

"I would not quite put it thus," I demurred. "It is my understanding that your Order has invested some little effort in researching ontological engineering."

"Some little effort, and some less results," he said with a dry chuckle.

"I believe that my knowledge of the field may serve to advance your position considerably."

"That would be of value to us. What do you want in return?"

"In addition to the room and board that have already been so generously extended to me, materials and facilities sufficient to construct a second ontological device, for my own purposes."

Purslaine nodded. "And what proof can you offer us of your knowledge or skill?"

"None but the thing itself," I demurred.

"Have you made an inventory of the materials you will require?"

I passed him two papers, covered in figures. "This is what I shall require for the engine," I explained, "and this for my own project."

He put on a pair of reading-glasses and set his cigar aside to pore over my figures for several minutes. At last he looked up and made as if to speak, but I held up one finger.

"I can build you an ontological engine, capable of such metamorphoses as might make Ovid gasp," I said. "I do not guarantee its safety or reliability. Ontological forces are difficult to harness, but nearly impossible to control."

"I think you for your honesty," he said.

I inclined my head.

"For so novel a project, I cannot endorse full payment in advance. I must request that you complete our Engine before you begin your own project. Is that acceptable to you?"

I thought for a moment. "That is extremely fair, Mr. President."

For the first time, he smiled: a great, frank grin that transformed his weathered face. "Excellent. Then good day to you, Mr. Dalrymple, and good luck."

The brother in charge of the laboratory was Dunlap, a tallish, stooped fellow, with extraordinarily thick spectacles, exceptionally pale skin, and curly golden locks in perpetual disarray.

As I began work on the engine, he provided—largely inadvertently—a rich vein of information on the state of ontological science in this world. "Of course! Brilliant!" he would say as I attached one set of components to the ever-growing engine. Then, "That will never work!" as I added another. His explanations of the latter were particularly fascinating. He has reached several eminently reasonably and fatally wrong conclusions about the nature of ontology that made it clear why their attempts at manipulating its forces had met with such an utter lack of success.

My days were consumed utterly by this work. I laboured long into the evening, attempting to flee the phantoms that pursued me the moment I put head to pillow in my little room upstairs at the club.

On the fifth night after my arrival, I had the basic circuits and amplifiers in place, though the fine control mechanisms that might allow the shaping of results (with the addition of a great deal of luck) still remained to be built and adjusted. I asked Weaver to attend at my first attempt at activation.

"Shouldn't there be some sort of ceremony? A ribbon-cutting or some such?"

"Not at all. The theory I know by heart, but I am not nearly so certain of my execution. I do not promise fireworks tonight, or, indeed, the next. The... er... the last project of this sort I worked on took weeks to render effective, and it only worked once before breaking down."

"Very well. I shall help howsoever I can."

Late that night, after I had gone minutely over each of the solders and clamps of my crude engine, I took a plum from my pocket and placed it upon the work-table. Then I handed the circlet to Weaver. "Be so good as to don this, if you please."

His nostrils flared as he took up the steel ring. "How strange is the human animal," he mused. "I feel a surge of excitement now, just taking up an erotofluidic collector."

"You've... served?"

"Oh, yes. My term ended about five years ago. It was a... a forma-tive experience." He donned the ring, and at once there was a faint play of blue light in a halo about his dark locks, flowing down into the Engine. I released a breath I had not known myself to be holding.

I positioned myself behind Weaver. He made as if to turn towards me, but I stayed his motion with a hand on his shoulder. Unlike Daedalus's engine, there were no knobs or switches on my makeshift device. It was turned on; now it wanted only power.

I took Weaver by the waist, my hands making free with his body. Through his waistcoat I could faintly feel the winding of thin linen which bound his bosom. One thumb stroked a nipple through all those layers of fabric.

The other delved within his trousers, creeping towards his genitals. After a week of near-complete deprivation, my own libido awoke with a start. I ground my rapidly swelling tool against his bottom, and he pressed back against it most eagerly.

When my fingertips reached Weaver's engorged labia, they an-nounced to me that he was indeed already in a state of considerable ex-citement. At the same time, my ears alerted me that the ontological energies gathered were nearing those sufficient to effect a transfor-mation. The faint whine of the Engine was rising in both pitch and volume, with a crackling sound now attending it.

I glanced at the parabola of the morphic projector and found that leaping cerulean lights were indeed flickering from one side to the other.

My hand emerged from his trousers. "Lick," I demanded, pressing my fingers to his lips, and he complied readily.

Once more I pressed my hand within, found his orifice, and pressed my fingertip against the very opening thereof. "Now watch," I said, pointing to my Engine.

I pushed my finger slowly inside my friend's slick opening, and as he groaned, a writhing beam of radiance fell from the collector onto the plum. Strange alterations in its colour and texture ensued; seams and ridges flowed and zig-zagged across it. My finger agitated within him; my palm pressed against his mons veneris.

Abruptly, the plum unfurled its leathery wings and sprung into the air, leaving behind a trail of sticky sweet-smelling droplets of juice.

It made directly for us, and Weaver uttered a vulgar word, then ducked, wrenching my hand painfully as it was pulled from his twat and his trousers. The transformed plum struck me full in the face, a flurry of membranous wings and aromatic pulp. I cried out in alarm, flailed my arms ineffectually about my head, and staggered back, trying to fend off the fast-moving abomination.

The subsequent few seconds are a blur in my recollection, but at their conclusion, Weaver held the plum at arm's length, its wings beating ineffectually against his wrist and forearm. The circlet had, in the excitement, fallen to the ground, and the engine was, without its power, inert once more. Even as I took in this sight, it altered, the wings shrinking and folding in upon themselves, until, in less time than it takes to write it, he held nothing more extraordinary or animate than a rather bruised plum in his extended fist.

Carefully, he returned the fruit, rather the worse for wear, to its previous place on the table. "This calls for a drink," he announced.

"For our nerves, or to celebrate?" I asked.

"Hmm. I wouldn't want to have to choose. Best make it a double then."

"Plum brandy?"

"Never again!"

I let Weaver get well into his whiskey before embarking on my tutorial on metaphysics. He gamely essayed to grasp my point.

"So these ontospheres," he said, waving his drink dangerously, "are entire... creations... with different inhabitants, possibly even different physical laws."

"Just so."

"Infinitely many."

"Precisely."

"But inaccessible."

"No."

He stared at me for a moment, then finished his drink in a single swallow.

"You've been to...?"

"You're getting warm."

"You're from...!"

I nodded.

He refilled our glasses. "Tell me all," he urged me.

"That will take time," I said.

"The night is young; the bottle is full. Tell me all."

When dawn's fingertips touched the horizon, we were standing out on the roof of the Brotherhood's meeting-house, taking in the morning air. "I see now why you seemed so remarkably ignorant in some ways, yet so puissant in others," Weaver mused. "What is your goal in our own world? Exploration? Conquest? Seduction?"

I laughed. "Originally exploration, I suppose. Now, escape. We had an equipment malfunction, and then an unfortunate run-in with an arbitor. Now, presumably, our Ontoscaphe has been seized by Her Majesty's agents."

"We?"

"My good friend Dewey came with me from our world. He provided a distraction to allow me to escape and was conscripted for his troubles."

Weaver looked rather solemn at the news. "That is rather a complication."

"Is there any possibility of your contacts within the——?"

He shook his head. "The government is extremely rigid upon that point. None shall be excused from service until the expiration of their full three years."

I nodded glumly. "The only thing that gives me hope is that we needn't maintain our fugitive status for long. If I can lay hands on him for but a minute, we can flee where they cannot follow. Now, you and I should go get a very good night's sleep. Our efforts resume tomorrow, but this time with an undertaking vastly more ambitious."

∾

I took the following morning off, wandering the streets of Manchester, taking the air and stretching my long-disused limbs.

That afternoon, Weaver had convened three distinguished members of the Order for decision making. Two Newbies stood attendance, maintaining the fire and suchlike.

Honouring my confidences, Weaver told an expurgated version of my tale: my apprenticeship with a secretive prodigy of ontological science, an ill-timed run-in with the Ministry, a hasty flight, a chance conversation on the locomotive.

He concluded with the tale of the previous night, how the device before us had transformed—temporarily—an ordinary plum into a flying fruity horror for several alarming minutes.

Oliphant, the order's secretary, cleared his throat. "Weaver, I hesitate to ask, but presented with such a tale, I find that I must: Was there laudanum involved in this remarkable adventure?"

Weaver coloured, the corners of his mouth turning down. "You think this was just a fancy? I did not imagine last night's events. Look, there is the monster itself!" He pointed with a flourish to the bruised plum which still rested on the work-table.

There was an uncomfortable silence.

Another of the gathering cleared his throat. "How was this device powered?"

"Erotofluidics," Weaver said quietly. "He, er, frigged me till I was near to spending."

There was another silence.

"He's rather good at it," he added defensively.

"Well," Oliphant said, "as I see it, there are two possibilities. One, begging your pardon, Weaver, is that the device is non-functional. There is some sort of fraud or error here. In that case, an attempt to use it for its intended purpose will simply fail, with no harm done beyond a certain degree of embarrassment for all concerned. The other is that it works, in which case, I, for one, am keen to move forward with all dispatch."

Purslaine looked grave but offered no objection to this line of reasoning.

Oliphant turned to Weaver, grinning. "Do we have a volunteer to power the engine?" he asked.

I would not have thought it possible for Weaver to blush further, but he managed to do so.

"This is rather more audience than I am entirely... er..."

"Such modesty! It is no matter. We shall have a junior member serve in your place."

He turned to me. "Mr. Dalrymple, it is necessary at this point to take you somewhat into our confidences. Our brotherhood, in addition to the good fellowship, mutual aid, and advocacy for violan causes that are our ostensible purposes, has certain pursuits about which we are more secretive. If I reveal these aspects to you, sir, may I rely upon your utmost discretion?"

"You may," I said, wondering wildly what secrets were about to be revealed to me.

"Our initiatory process contains elements that... might be considered indecent by the world at large."

"Indecent," I said. "You mean you fuck the initiates?"

"Well, in a manner of—"

"And flog them, too, I'll be bound."

"Yes...."

"I do hope there's more to this deep, dark secret."

There was an uncomfortable silence.

"Very well, then," I said briskly. "I hereby promise to be discreet about this shameful, deep, dark secret, which is certainly unique in all the annals of gentlemen's clubs."

I returned to my labours, the work now more exacting and exhausting than ever, as now it was not simply a question of getting the device to work, but of getting it to work well. Another week of maddeningly precise work passed.

I awoke with a start, looking about myself wildly, through sleep-clogged eyes, for the cause of my panic. There was an intruder in the laboratory! I lurched to my feet and grabbed the nearest weapon with which to defend myself and my creations.

"Dalrymple, my dear fellow," Weaver—for it was he—said. "This schedule to which you are holding yourself is entirely unsustainable."

I blinked several times, attempting to focus on his visage.

"Look at you! You haven't shaved in a week, and you seem to be attempting to threaten me with last week's newspaper. You've slept, what, three hours in the last forty-eight?"

I consulted my pocket watch, only to find that it had run down. "Five, at least," I corrected him. "The sun was barely up when I fell asleep this morning."

"Seven, then, and a fraction. But I must implore you to take a sab-bath day!"

"Very well," I said.

"As your friend, and as a representative of—Wait, you agree?"

"Certainly."

"I confess that I expected you to show more recalcitrance."

"The Engine is complete."

"Capital news! You've tested it? It is working?"

"I did."

"How?"

"I set it to transform a cabbage into a cucumber."

"And you were successful?"

"Er... yes."

"But?"

"Cucumbers do not traditionally have pincers, I believe."

"That is my understanding as well. And it helps explain the wad of bandages about your finger. Do you need salve? A large fly swatter?"

"The uncharacteristically aggressive cucumber is now safely settled in one of the terraria. I wonder what I should be feeding it...?"

"As fascinating as that question is, I shall set it aside for the nonce to raise one perhaps even more urgent: do you really think the device is ready?"

"Weaver, my dear fellow, I cannot advocate the Engine's use on human subjects. The technology is still young and little understood, and, frankly, I question whether ontological forces can ever be entirely tamed. There is a turbulent, chaotic quality to these energies that seems to me to dwell within their very nature.

"What I can tell you is that I have done my very best. The Engine is as sound, and as safe, as I can make it, and if your brothers are set in their resolve to undergo its emanations, I shall do my best to see them through it."

"I had hoped to sway you with my own persuasive powers, but that will do, to be sure. I advise you to rest up, then, for tonight is a meeting of the brotherhood to which I have won you a special invitation."

"I confess that I neglected to pack evening-clothes when travelling to this ontosphere."

"You rest up," Weaver urged me. "I shall attend to attire."

Weaver leading, we descended to the club's basement, an area I had never before laid eyes upon. "Welcome to the Brotherhood's Snuggery," he said, as we ducked our heads to pass through the low doorway. "It is a rare privilege for us to allow a non-member at these little gatherings."

As my eyes adjusted to the relative darkness, my other senses leapt to compensate. The air was a little close and warm, notes of perspiration and female excitement perceptible beneath the smoke from the massive fireplace that cast most of the room's illumination.

From every quarter came moans, whimpers, cries, groans, liquid sloshing sounds, and sharp percussions. Junior brothers of the Order of St. Joan stood, crouched, reclined, crawled, and hung suspended in dazzling array, most of them entirely nude. It struck me that, even unclothed, their attitudes and bearings marked them as something other than ordinary women of my own ontosphere.

Four violas hung in the centre of the room, suspended from their wrists and ankles, serving as sort of erotofluidic candelabra, blue light playing about the collections circuits above their heads. From time to time, when the illumination of one or the other would flag, a fully-clothed senior member would wander over and, with remorselessly probing fingers, tease him back to writhing, whimpering radiance once again.

As my eyes became accustomed to the darkness, they hungrily drank in the array of fascinating sights about me. By the door, three Newbertons were bent over a single camel-hair sofa, their uplifted bottoms presenting a pleasing diversity of shapes, tho' the senior brother, paddle in hand, appeared to be working towards a uniformity of hue, pausing often to survey the three unhappily wriggling posteriors with a critical eye, before landing a flurry of blows on the palest, to the bearer's noisy distress, and his companions' momentary relief.

Another sofa had another three initiates in like position, but, of these, two were being vigourously fucked by senior members with ivory godemiches strapped over their trousers, while a third had a brother crouched between his thighs, feasting hungrily. Even in the meeting room's uncertain light, it was clear that all three had previously undergone like treatment to their brothers, their bottoms still blushing from a vigourous recent spanking.

One Newbie lay in a mound of pillows on the floor, legs resting on the shoulders of a senior brother, who had four fingers pressed into his cunt, and seemed to be in the process of introducing his thumb. The initiate's cries were intermittently stifled by the kisses from another brother, in whose lap his head rested, and who alternated tenderly stroking his face and tugging at his nipples in a manner that wrung desperate shouts from the helpless victim's throat.

Weaver stood silent at my side, giving me a minute to absorb the remarkable tableau, of which I have described only a tenth part above. "Weaver," I said after a time, "I owe Mr. Purslaine an apology. This is indeed a level of debauchery to be proud of. My dismissiveness was premature and ignorant."

Weaver grinned. "You are too kind, Dalrymple. Here, let me show you about."

Along the wall, a half-dozen naked Newbies squirmed, with expressions of mixed desire and discomfort. Further scrutiny revealed that they were impaled, to a man, on a series of curving shafts that emerged from the wall at a suitable height.

"A little low for a hat-rack, what?" I observed.

Weaver nodded. "And a little high for a shoe-tree. So we find what purposes we can."

A brother I had not met prowled back and forth before the Newbies. One, whose energy seemed to be flagging a bit, he favoured with a passionate kiss, in the midst of which he gripped his victims hips and thrust him down onto the spike that impaled him. A muffled howl emerged from their locked lips. When they parted, the nude initiate was grinding vigourously against the wall-mounted cock.

The Newb next to him appeared to find this display particularly inspiring, biting his lip to suppress his own cries as his undulations increased in speed and vigour. A climax seemed imminent at the moment before he was plucked off his mount and thrown across the monitor's lap. He yowled and kicked vigourously as he received what was clearly not the first thorough spanking of his evening.

Dropped onto the gleaming shaft once more, the Newberton blinked his glistening eyes rapidly, his thighs trembling with the effort to hold his hips still under his master's watchful eyes.

"So they are to remain excited," I surmised aloud, "but are forbidden to spend."

"Precisely," Weaver said, "keeping them in an optimal state should any brother wish to make use of them at any moment. Are you up for a little sport?"

"Always."

"Excellent." He had a moment's whispered consultation with the brother, who then accompanied him to stand before the Newb at the leftmost end.

Said initiate was rocking himself upon the shaft he bestrode with slow, shuddering motions, eyes shut with concentration. He was slender and extremely fair, with small breasts and aquiline features. Standing erect, he was a few inches taller than Weaver; when crouching to impale himself, they were of a height.

At one such nadir, Weaver spoke softly: "David."

The Newberton opened his eyes and froze in place. "Mr. Weaver."

"I have a friend I wish to introduce you to. Dismount."

Once David had stumbled off the platform, he stood with his arms crossed behind him, which served to display his small, large-nippled bosoms to fine effect. Weaver pressed gently on one shoulder, and he dropped to his knees with practised grace, each hand still gripping the opposite elbow behind his back.

"Victor, this is my protégé, David Van Horn."

"A pleasure to make your acquaintance," I said.

The Newbie on his knees glanced up at my face, and, when our eyes met, I sensed, for an instant, the frustration and hunger that the Brotherhood of St. Joan had so carefully and mercilessly cultivated in him. "Thank you, sir," he said simply.

Weaver put his arm about my waist. "David has been an exceptional student," he murmured into my ear, his hot breath making the hairs on the back of my neck stand up. "Submissive, indefatigable, spirited, and a truly voracious cock-sucker."

Already rosy-cheeked, David coloured still further at these words. "You are very kind, sir," he said.

Weaver sighed. "I try not to be, but accidents do happen." He continued: "Mr. Dalrymple here is quite the connoisseur of that last skill. If he permits, you are to demonstrate your mastery of it for him."

David nodded minutely. "Thank you, sir."

Then he looked up at me with great, pale blue eyes. "Please, Mr. Dalrymple, sir, may I give you a suck?"

At this plea, my cock leapt involuntarily, and the Newbie twitched, apparently startled by the sight. One of Weaver's hands was about my waist. The other grasped my tool firmly through my trousers, sending a wave of pleasure through me. His hand then proceeded to the buttons of my fly, working with a maddening leisureliness to free my pego from its close confinement.

David whimpered and squirmed at my feet, trying desperately to catch Weaver's eye, apparently keen for permission to speak. The latter ignored his protégé's discomfort, reaching into my trousers and running a thumb over the wet head of my cock, only to withdraw his hand again and press the thumb into David's mouth. He smiled as

David shuddered with suppressed emotion, sucking frantically at the proffered digit, as if striving to induce it to ejaculate more of the fluid he had just sampled.

His other hand left my waist and quested, somewhat more awkwardly, within my open fly. With no small effort, he pulled my rigid pego into view, just as he removed his hand from David's mouth.

"Oh my goodness," the kneeling viola breathed, "it is a real co—!" But before he could finish his sentence, Weaver had gripped a handful of hair and pulled his head back to look him directly in the eye.

"A what?" Weaver said sternly.

"A-a-a flesh cock," David stammered.

"Better." He slacked his grip on David's hair somewhat but did not release him. The Newb's head rolled forward again, so that his half-open lips breathed warm, moist air on the head of my member. Weaver squeezed the base, and I sighed with pleasure. The head of my cock swelled, the fine reticulations of the surface smoothing as the bulb inflated and darkened. A fresh clear drop appeared at the tip.

Weaver wielded my cock like a paintbrush, running the fluid across David's trembling lower lip while his other hand continued to hold David's head in place. A small noise escaped the boy's throat.

"Smell," Weaver ordered, and David's delicate nostrils flared. He whimpered again on the exhale, and something tense in him relaxed, his shoulders moving back and down with the breath.

"Now lick."

David brought his pointed tongue to the head of my cock, and for a moment a groan was audible from his throat, before my own louder expression of pleasure drowned it out.

Weaver released the Newbie's hair and the base of my cock, apparently feeling that the processes he had set in motion had now acquired their own momentum.

"Now suck," he ordered, and David drew a deep breath and took the head of my cock in his hot mouth. He slid down deliberately until the head was firmly pressed against his soft palate, then held there, his lips working as if striving to draw in the remaining inch of my shaft.

He drew back and gulped for breath, his eyes flickering from

Weaver's face to my own. It seemed the moment to take a more active role in the proceedings. "An excellent beginning," I praised him, and he beamed with pride, but only for an instant, before my hand on the back of his head was urging forward again, this time meeting a thrust of my hips as I began to make use of that beguiling orifice in earnest.

My groans of pleasure filled my own ears, counterpointed by the kneeling Newbie's gulps and gasps. And, underneath both, Weaver's happy purr as he leaned in to share, as much as possible, my own view of my rigid shaft penetrating his protégé's mouth.

As my own excitement grew, I took hold of two handfuls of David's hair. He whimpered piteously in a way I found particularly delightful, so I tightened my grip, and was rewarded with a shudder running all the way down his body. I pulled his head off of my cock by this grip, with an audible pop, and gazed down at his face. His face was flushed, his eyes unfocused. A few bubbles of saliva slowly slid down his chin. He cried out—short, soft calls, like a new-hatched sparrow clamouring for more worms.

Accordingly, I fed him the worm he so craved, bringing his face down onto my prick, and holding it in place for me to fuck into, each thrust provoking a muffled cry. During the interludes in which neither of us was calling aloud, I could hear his rapid, deep breathing through his nostrils.

Releasing me from his half-embrace, Weaver crouched beside us and ran his hand down David's back, his hand disappearing from view beneath the kneeling Newbie, who gave forth a long, loud groan. "Bl—dy h—l, is he wet," Weaver confided to me, the muscles in his forearm flexing rhythmically.

David's diminished attentiveness to suction was compensated for by the exquisite vibrations, as he attempted to cry out with my cock lodged halfway down his throat.

Weaver noted my own answering yell, and the attendant acceleration in my digs at David's mouth. "That's it, Dalrymple," he urged me on, "give the little bugger a good mouthful."

To the boy, however, he urged restraint: "Not yet, not yet. A good little Newbie doesn't spend till he's told." David undulated his bottom lasciviously, striving to gain more penetration, more friction from Weaver's cunningly teasing fingers, which withdrew however much David should reach for them.

I reached the short digs, cried out, and gripped David's hair so forcefully it must have caused the poor boy real pain.

"Now," Weaver said, and his arm went forward. David began wailing, a sound interrupted by coughing and sputtering as I ejaculated down his throat. I withdrew my cock for fear of an involuntary bite and stroked myself to the completion of my orgasm, spurting my last few drops onto the Newberton's flushed face as he continued to alternate howls of pleasure and coughing fits.

With watery legs, I staggered to a nearby easy chair and slumped, temporarily spent.

No such exhaustion appeared to obtain for the other two, however. David's cheek was now pressed to the cushion beneath him, his bottom elevated and waggling lasciviously, as Weaver saw to him with a will, the sloshing noise of his fingers within the Newbie's cunny carrying easily even over his cries, no longer muffled but now clear and sharp, as well as the range of noises from similar undertakings throughout the room. Weaver maintained a steady stream of vile epithets and implausible threats as he worked more and more of his hand into his protégé's cunt, each sentence provoking another wail of submission and need.

In scant minutes, the Newbie's whole body froze in place, deep groans wrenched from him with each thrust of his master's arm, and he finally collapsed to the cushion, spent. Weaver stood, breathing a little heavily, forehead gleaming with perspiration, a fierce happy grin illuminating his visage. He gave David a few moments of respite, then ordered, "Undress me."

If David was perhaps sluggish, even languid in responding to the command, if he showed uncharacteristic clumsiness with the laces and buttons of his master's attire, Weaver was inclined to be lenient for the moment. I glanced about and saw that throughout the busy room, members' attire had diminished to more nearly match that of the Newbies, still easily distinguishable by their collars, and by their uniformly glowing bottoms.

As David unwound the linen straps that bound Weaver's bosom, I realized that I had never seen him entirely *au naturale* before.

The breasts revealed were heavy and soft, with broad, dark nipples. I was hard once more, painfully so.

Naked, Weaver strode to me, pulling David along with a gentle tug at his hair, and gestured for me to stand. I did so and stripped, as rapidly as I could, until I was as naked as my friend, who bade me sit once more.

David had a French letter, acquired I know not when, which he slipped onto my prick, then Weaver straddled me, his soft bosom brushing my face. I felt a cool, slender hand—David's—gripping the base of my cock, angling me just so, then powerful heat, delicious compression, exquisite weight as Weaver settled himself onto me, lips meeting mine in a sustained kiss.

We coupled thus, slowly, for a long time, David's questing tongue on my cods and Weaver's bottom-hole sending thrills up our spines as we enjoyed each other, alternating long, slow kisses with enjoyment of the numerous piquant sights the rest of the room had to offer. At last, Weaver reached between our pressed-together bodies to stroke his clitoris until his vagina fluttered upon my shaft, provoking in turn my own answering orgasm.

After a few minutes, we disentangled. I had barely the energy to gather up my clothes, shake my friend's hand very warmly, thanking him for a memorable evening, and, assured of the safety of such, make my way, naked, back to my bedroom to fall into a deep slumber.

I presented the case to the senior brothers the next day, at the foot of a long mahogany table. In front of me rested the terrarium, wherein the cucumber waved its horny pincers menacingly at the assembled sages. I felt a duty to impress upon them the hazards of the undertaking, and my warty green friend seemed an effective visual aid to that end.

Of the dozen violas gathered, five desired the treatment, the other seven finding the bodies they currently possessed satisfactory, at least with regard to sex.

The consensus of the meeting was to proceed with the undertaking. "Who, then, shall be our first subject?" said President Purslaine.

There was a moment's silence. From Purslaine's left hand, Brother Oliphant paused in his scribbling and spoke softly: "I will."

Purslaine's eyes widened a bit. "Let the record so show," he said. "I believe that calling for a second volunteer before the disposition of Brother Oliphant's case would be premature. Therefore, if there is no further business...?" He paused for a moment before resuming. "This meeting is adjourned until the morrow."

Chapter 5: The Ontological Engine

That night at supper, I could barely bring myself to eat a bite. So much hung upon the outcome of that evening: my pride as an ontological engineer not trivial, but not less my own fate, Dewey's, and the well-being of the person subjecting himself to the Engine's volatile rays.

Oliphant drank rather more claret than was his habit, and his cheeks became a bit more flushed than might ordinarily be seen, but otherwise he was his steady, imperturbable self.

Though no announcement had been made to the brotherhood at large, an indefinable air of excitement was to be felt at the banquet table. At the meal's close, Purslaine stood, and all fell silent at once for his speech. This, I suspect, was as much due to his personality as his office; he was not a man given to unnecessary verbiage, nor one fond of having his time wasted.

"The Erotofluidic Committee will be testing a new device," he announced crisply. At once a wave of murmurs passed through the junior brothers. "Service as a power-source will of course be painful and humiliating. There may, additionally, be an element of danger in this instance."

He paused to sip his sherry.

"Have I any volunteers?"

All hands rose as if by one will.

"So eager?" I whispered to Weaver.

"They are dying to know what you have been working on," he murmured back. "Whoever gains that intelligence first will be considerably elevated amongst his peers."

"Norris," Purslaine said, pointing to one of the Newbertons. "You are excused from table. Report to Dunlap in the laboratory."

In all too little time, we followed the intrepid Norris into the bowels of the building. I was consumed with trepidation—had I managed to fully impress on the Joanites, on Oliphant himself, the hazards of the undertaking? Could I refuse this task? No: they were entering into it of their own free wills. They were being men of their words; could I be less?

I had spent a half-hour shoving debris—both my own and the Brotherhood's—to one wall or the other to make room for the anticipated gathering. Dunlap had undone a portion of this, extracting one curious device from the mounded scree. It was reminiscent of Daedalus's rather sinister Collection Stands, and indeed proved to be akin in function. The sight that greeted our eyes as we entered the room was a broad white posterior, which in time proved to be Norris's, that wriggled and twitched, its bearer crouched over a padded bench and secured at wrists and ankles, his head somewhat lower than his hips.

A low buzzing signified the presence of a Vibratorium, and, given the way Norris squirmed against the bench, striving to maximize its contact with his clitoris, it was evident that it was thence that the sound emanated.

As each of the Board members filed in, he would pat Norris's bottom familiarly, many murmuring a word or two to him. He stiffened at this treatment, evidently feeling anew the indignity of his position now that his audience was greatly expanded, but his determination to restrain his movements lasted only a couple of minutes. In little time, he was undulating against the bench with renewed fervour, his whimpers reflecting, in their elevated pitch, the sharpened humiliation of his circumstances.

It was only now that I noted a crucial point of difference between Daedalus's Collection Stands and the device that confined poor Norris. Whereas the former contraption demanded constant involvement from its operator, Dunlap stood, monitoring the dials with his hands clasped behind his back.

I walked over to observe his work more closely and inquired about the lack of oversight.

"Ah, that is an innovation of my own," Dunlap explained, with evident pride. "Watch!"

Norris's motions were becoming increasingly animated, his cries rising in pitch. As his legs started to tremble, the hum of the Vibratorium abruptly cut off. His undulations only became more frantic, his cries more desperate, as he attempted to coax enough friction from the bench's cushion to allow the climax he so urgently craved.

At last, he slumped downward in defeat. A moment later, the hum of the Vibratorium resumed.

Dunlap was grinning at me.

"A cut-off switch!" I said. "Ingenious!"

"It's really terribly simple," he said modestly, "but the effect is quite gratifying. My self-regulating Erotofluidic Tantalizer can keep a subject in a state of the most exquisite frustration for hours. The moment his erotic output exceeds a certain level, the stimulation ends. When his excitement subsides, it resumes." He glanced appraisingly down at the distended front of my trousers. "I see your appreciation of the effect is not purely intellectual." He reached out and ran a thumb along the length of my rigid cock. "Perhaps you would be available to assist me in modifying the device to work with anatomy such as yours at some time?"

I glanced back at poor Norris, who appeared to be once again struggling to resist the lure of the vibrations against his clitoris, a struggle he was slowly losing as his traitorous body demanded further stimulation. Trails of perspiration ran down his thighs and back, though the room was not particularly warm, and the aroma of his excitement was faintly perceptible through the reek of machine oil and the ozone tang of erotofluidic energies. "Perhaps," I said cautiously.

Oliphant's expression was characteristically stoical, but his complexion was faintly tinged with green, and he kept largely to himself as the group circulated and discussed the forthcoming experiment. More than once, when he thought no-one was looking, I saw his eyes drift towards the terrarium, where that singularly aggressive cucumber waved its pincers menacingly at the assembled throng. Not wishing to prolong the poor man's agony of anticipation any further, I gathered up Dunlap and enlisted his aid in hooking up his ingeniously perverse collection device to my Ontological Engine.

As the circuit was completed, the engine began to hum, a deep, throbbing noise that brought the room to an immediate hush, through which one could clearly discern the higher-pitched buzz of the Vibratorium and the continued whimpers of poor Norris atop it.

"Mr. Oliphant, if you please," I said, and gestured towards the seat of honour. As this Engine was designed specifically with operation upon human subjects in mind, in place of Daedalus's work-table, I had requisitioned a handsome leather easy-chair from downstairs. In that, Oliphant seated himself, his face a studied mask of calm, but his knuckles whitened upon the arms of the chair.

I nodded to Dunlap, who turned a dial. The hum of the Vibratorium rose to an angry whine. Norris's cries rose in pitch and volume, until one brother strode over and, not ungently, clapped a hand over the mouth of the Newberton, an act which served to grant him further license so that Norris thrashed and screamed against his elder brother's palm as the climax arrived which he had sought so desperately for so long.

Nary a glance did he receive, though, from the members of the Ontological Committee, as a halo of cerulean luminosity descended about Brother Oliphant. "Oh!" he exclaimed, "Oh my!" as a writhing penumbra of radiance formed about his temple. "What a curious sensation! It's as if I—I—" and he sneezed, thrice, in rapid succession, great honking sneezes that had him squirming about in his chair to extract a pocked handkerchief.

He blew his nose noisily and copiously, and then, as if by life-long instinct, carefully smoothed down the luxuriant moustache and great square beard that had not been there the moment before. Only then did a look of wonderment steal over his face, as he felt with the other hand at his new whiskers.

Already the radiance about him was dying away as Norris's climax subsided, leaving the Newbie spent and panting upon the Collection Stand and the secretary of the Brotherhood of St. Joan twitching impatiently in his seat. "A glass!" he cried out in a voice substantially deeper and richer than he had possessed the moment before. "I must have a looking-glass!"

The moment the ontological radiance had subsided completely, he sprang from his seat to rummage through the cluttered corners of the room, until he found a small, round looking-glass, into which he peered eagerly.

"Elias," Purslaine said, "how do you feel?"

"Good, good," Oliphant answered abstractedly, stroking his beard in the glass with evident pleasure. Then, apparently realizing a fuller response was called for, he turned to face the Committee full on. He was, in every visible respect, unmistakably the brother of the viola who had entered the room. His features were coarser and stronger than they had been. He was of a like stoutness to his previous form, though rather less at the hip and bosom, and rather more at the belly than before, such that the suit which previously had fit him admirably was now pulled taut across the front.

"Excellent, in fact," Oliphant continued his self-assessment. "And... rather randy."

"Well, lets see it," Purslaine said.

"See what?"

"The goods," Purslaine said impatiently. "The meat and two veg, the staff and the orbs, the cabbages and cod."

"You wish me to take down my trousers and display my genitals to the Committee?"

Purslaine smiled lopsidedly. "For science!"

"For science!" Oliphant agreed, and began unfastening his trousers. When he had several buttons open, he reached inside to give himself a head-start, as it were, on the discoveries he was about to share with his brothers.

A remarkable series of emotions succeeded each other across his visage: alarm, confusion, amazement. His hand worked busily, exploring the parts within for a full minute.

"Well, don't just stand there wanking yourself," Purslaine interrupted him testily. "Lets have a look!"

Oliphant unfastened his final trouser button, and the garment fell to his knees. From his groin jutted an appendage of prodigious length, greyish and wrinkled. As Oliphant's eyes fell upon it, he emitted a small cry of startlement, and the limb itself twitched from a downward curve to an upward one, revealing two largish orifices at its apex. It was only then that I recognized it as elephant's trunk, transplanted, in miniature, to the Joanite's nether parts.

There was perfect silence, the gathering of distinguished violas struck dumb. In that stillness, Oliphant's protuberance flexed slowly to the left, until it was nearly bent double. Then, with a slowly-dawning smile of satisfaction, he bent it back the other way.

Oliphant reached into his waistcoat pocket and withdrew a fine gold watch, which he held out in one cupped hand. His extraordinary protuberance nosed clumsily against it several times before successfully gripping the timepiece, lifting it, and then flipping the cover open. At last it stretched upward and deposited Oliphant's watch back in its pocket.

Oliphant threw back his head and roared in a booming tenor: "Success!"

The room erupted into a buzz of agitated voices as every Joanite turned to discuss the event with his fellow.

All at once, Oliphant was down from the stage, his trousers still bunched at his thighs, pumping my hand in his own two broad mitts, tears of joy running down his face to disappear into his beard. "Extraordinary! Extraordinary! I never imagined! It's just... extraordinary!" he babbled. Even through the surprise of this development and the pain of his powerful grip on my hand, his enthusiasm was infectious, and my answering smile was genuine.

His voice dropped, and he leaned in. "When will it be... ready? Safe to use?" As he spoke, his trunk, still protruding from his trousers, rose and probed the air, its nostrils flaring.

With an effort, I broke my gaze from the sight to look him in the eye. "Erm... you mean...?

He nodded. "Fucking!"

"Immediately, to the best of my knowledge. I really know little more than you do in this case."

"Excellent!" He sprang back to his chair and began unlacing his boots.

For my own part, I found a stool by the Engine, and sat, working through the operations of the engine in my mind.

From behind me came Dunlap's voice: "The morphic stabilizers?"

I nodded. "Just a quarter-turn tighter, I should think. Too far, and there's no ontological displacement at all. Care to lend a hand?"

"Let me just get my tool kit."

On the stage, Oliphant was by now entirely in a state of nature, or, rather, entirely unclothed, nature having little enough to do with the body he now inhabited with such evident comfort.

He crooked a finger, his member echoing the gesture, and Norris, equally nude but far more self conscious, mounted the low stage, crossing his arms under his considerable breasts.

"Norris, are you up to assisting me with one more little scientific experiment?" Oliphant said, not ungently.

Norris murmured something.

"Speak up, young fellow," Oliphant admonished him. "The gentlemen in the back row are going to have trouble hearing you."

Norris glanced round at the crowd that watched him intently and flushed further. "I shall endeavour to accommodate all of your..." he looked once more at the member that reached up past its owner's navel, swaying back and forth in a king cobra's hypnotic undulations, "...your needs, Mr. Oliphant."

"Good, brave lad," Oliphant said soothingly. "Let us then hie ourselves to the snuggery!"

"Hurrah!" came the general cry from the assembled worthies. "Onward to the snuggery!"

Dunlap clapped a hand on my shoulder. "Ready!" he announced. As the rest of the gathering processed raucously out the door, we set to work.

A good hour of delicate tinkering later, I leaned back, reasonably satisfied.

"You know," I mused, "my old mentor, Daedalus Tesla, used to insist that men and women produced palpably different varieties of erotofluidic emanations."

Dunlap cocked an eyebrow sceptically. "And violas?"

"Do not exist in my ontosphere."

He opened his mouth, about to embark on a disquisition upon one of his favoured topics: the secret violan history of the world. Among the figures he claimed as antecedents were Charlemagne, Michelangelo, and several popes, in addition to St. Joan, Queen Elizabeth, and numerous figures of lesser notability. It had been an interesting enough subject the first two or three times, but I did not look forward to a fourth with pleasure.

"Not publicly in my ontosphere," I conceded hastily. "To be quite honest, I never observed the differences that Daedalus did."

"Do you think men and women are different here than there, then?"

"Actually, I suspect that Daedalus's engine had an unreliable stabilization array, but Daedalus saw what he wished to see. A great mind, to be sure, but not without his blind spots."

Dunlap and I emerged from the laboratory to find the snuggery's festivities still vigourously under way. We shook hands goodnight, and he went to join in the debauchery while I staggered off to bed.

The next morning, I was in no fit state for conversation, still blinking blearily into my first cup of tea, while Weaver was rhapsodising about the epic debaucheries of the night before. Apparently, Oliphant's prehensile organ had reduced no fewer than four Newbies and two full brothers to near-insensate quivering orgasmic masses before the order's secretary was himself exhausted. Nor was that the end of the evening, as one more brother availed himself of the slumbering Oliphant's yet-intrepid trunk for a further round.

Weaver leaned in close. "What's your intent for Murchison?" he asked. "A rhinoceros horn? A monkey's paw? Perhaps a tentacle from a great sea...."

Noticing my expression, his fantasia ground to an awkward halt.

"Oliphant loves his new cock," he said more seriously, "even if it isn't precisely standard-issue. In fact, I rather think he favours it more than he would an ordinary one. All evening he was showing everyone he could get to stand still that trick with the pocket watch."

I digested this a moment. "He kept his waistcoat on all evening?"

"He put it back on, after he'd otherwise disrobed. The effect was rather incongruous."

"I should think. And Murchison? What did he think of Oliphant's trunk?"

"Murchison was looking a little green about the gills last night, I do concede. He is still determined though, despite the risks."

That afternoon, we assembled once more in the laboratory, a fresh Newbie strapped into the stimulator. Lacking appetite for lunch, I had spent the past hour checking over the connections on the engine, determined to do whatever was possible to avert excessive ontological displacement in my next subject, who might not prove as flexible in his consideration of what was an enhancement and what was a disfigurement.

Murchison was a tallish fellow, with a high forehead, a strong nose, and dark, deep-set, glittering eyes. He took my shoulder in one long hand and spoke softly to me: "Mr. Dalrymple, I want you to know, that, whatever should transpire this afternoon, I consider you a great benefactor to myself and to the brotherhood. I am well aware that ontological engineering is not yet an exact art, and I undertake that risk knowingly. What we shall attempt today is what I have ardently desired for myself for a great many years. I thank you for this opportunity."

I stammered out some words of acknowledgement, moved almost to tears by this bold ontonaut's intense emotion and seriousness of purpose.

He sat in the chair; the crowd fell silent, the hum of the engine and the Newbie's rhythmic yelping the room's only sounds. I nodded to

Dunlap, who disengaged the tantalization cut-off, propelling the Newberton towards the climax it had been deferring. Then I turned the
dial, allowing the ontological energies to surge through the Engine.
The machine's throbbing whine rose in pitch and volume, and blue
florescence flickered down the circuit, tiny crackling vortices of
cerulean radiance spiralling off the parabolic collector. As the light
cast his features into dramatic relief, Murchison sat up a bit straighter,
the hairs on his head standing out a little from the charge upon them.

"Stop!" he cried out abruptly. "Stop!"

At once Dunlap yanked the cord harnessing the Tantalizer to the
Engine, and, deprived of power, the Engine subsided to stillness.

There was a moment's silence.

"What happened?" said Purslaine.

"I... I changed my mind," Murchison said.

"You what?"

"I changed my mind."

"You decided the risk was too much?"

"No, no, not at all. I realized that I don't want the change, even if
it's a perfect success."

"You don't?"

"No... I always thought I did. It always felt like what I craved, but
then, when I finally felt that it was really about to happen, I...."

He fell silent.

"You preferred what you have," Purslaine ventured.

"Just so."

"Well, then. I suppose, in a sense, you got what you needed, even
if it was just a chance to know that it was a real choice."

Murchison looked about at all the uncertain faces about him, and
his own face, which had been the very picture of perplexity, resolved
into an expression of dismay. "You must all think me a terrible cow-
ard," he said. "And I suppose you are correct."

There was a moment's uncertain silence, and then a voice from
the back of the room began to sing, a little hesitantly: "For he's a jolly
good fellow...."

By the end of the second line, several others had taken it up. By the
end of the third, the room was booming with dozens of voices: "And

nobody can deny! And nobody can deny!"

They filed out, jostling and singing raucously, clapping Murchison on the back, and embracing him warmly. In scant minutes, only Dunlap, myself, and the whimpering Newbie remained in the room.

"Did you do that?" Dunlap said. "I mean, was that change natural... or... induced?"

"I haven't the foggiest," I answered, quite truthfully.

"Well, I could use a drink," Dunlap said, standing and dusting his hands. "Care to join me?"

"Why not?" I said.

The following afternoon, I consulted with Dunlap at some length about what modifications to the Engine, if any, might be called for after the ambiguous case of Murchison. It is the nature of ontological energies to render fine control by the engineer problematic at best. It is a force that operates by its own perverse logic, and, as no two subjects are perfectly identical, the results of an ontological operation can never be perfectly replicated. We contented ourselves with a cautious tuning up of the morphic stabilizers, then joined the masses already gathering for supper.

The third volunteer was Nigel Stafford, a cheery and gregarious fellow who was a particular friend of President Purslaine.

Dunlap took me aside. "Our Newbie today is Giddings. It's a miracle he hasn't served yet—he's a seven at least."

"Meaning?"

"Have you ever worked with an erotic prodigy? It has distinctive hazards to the equipment."

"And to the engineer," I agreed.

His eyes widened, and he nodded slowly. "Potentially," he admitted.

"This is an area in which your knowledge is greater than mine," I said. "Can you limit how much power goes to the engine?"

"Certainly."

"Then that may be for the best."

Where Oliphant and Murchison had been distinctly inward in their anxiety, Stafford was all excess of energy, laughing loudly, striding back and forth, drumming his fingertips upon every available surface. In time, we got him settled on the chair, where he tapped his foot impatiently, his hands working in his lap. "Well, get on with it," he called out jocularly. "At this rate, I shall be late for the nine o'clock whist tournament!"

I nodded to Dunlap, who turned the dial, accelerating the stimulation of the notorious Giddings. As anticipated, the needle on the erotometer built into the engine neared its limit nearly at once. The smell of ozone began to suffuse the room. I glanced once more at Stafford, who gave an impatient get-on-with-it gesture with one hand. I pulled the lever, and blue radiance flowed from Giddings through the Collector to the Engine, where it eddied in the categoric multipliers, and then poured, with redoubled radiance, onto the Brotherhood's volunteer.

He froze in place and seemed almost to glow from within, his eyes wide as the wild ontological energies pervaded his body, acting not just upon his body or his spirit, but upon his very nature. Whatever transformations were occurring, however, had as yet left no visible mark. Giddings climaxed noisily, and nearly at once began the ascent towards another such. I gestured to Dunlap to increase the flow of erotic force. The radiance in the room intensified. The ontological forces striking Stafford threatened to break off into vortices such as those that had once wreaked such havoc in Daedalus's laboratory, but the more-refined form of the projectors kept the forces focused on Stafford. Still, no change was visible in his face or form, however.

"More," I called to Dunlap. The sound and lights increased in intensity.

"That's all of it," he said at last, shouting to be heard over the throbbing of the engine and the crackling of the ontological power that flowed about Stafford.

Giddings attained another climax, and the ozone smell of the engine was joined by a harsher smell as cables overheated under the elevated erotofluidic load.

Stafford convulsed with a single strangled cry, and I cut the power.

He stood then, even as the radiance about him was fading, and it was apparent that he had gained several inches in height, his clothes this time altering along with him, so that they fit him as well as ever. He had additionally acquired a moustache, impeccably curled and waxed, which he smoothed absent-mindedly as he looked about himself.

"Nigel! How do you feel?" Purslaine asked anxiously.

"Fine, fine," Stafford answered. "Yourself?"

"Well, lets see it, then!"

Stafford looked utterly perplexed. "See what?"

"Your genitals!"

Stafford drew back and flushed darkly. "I beg your pardon?"

"It's for sci—" Purslaine began, but seeing the younger man's expression, he changed tacks. "Are you certain you're all right, Nigel?"

"I am perfectly fine," Stafford answered acerbically. "Now if you could tell me who you are, and what this place is, without demanding any further obscene indignities of me at the same time, I should be much obliged."

Purslaine took a deep breath before answering: "I am your friend Walter Purslaine. This is your club, the Brotherhood of St. Joan. You are not well, Nigel. Seat yourself and rest."

"So you can attempt to examine my genitals again? Thank you very much, but I shall decline your gracious offer, Mr. Purslaine. And, now, if you do not wish to find yourself before a magistrate for kidnapping, I would urge you to show me the way out of this so-called club with all haste."

"Nigel. Please—" Purslaine attempted to remonstrate.

"The door, Mr. Purslaine."

Purslaine's shoulders slumped. "Hastings, show the gentleman out," he said.

With a final haughty glance about the room, Stafford exited.

∾

There were no celebrations that evening.

Quite late, I found President Purslaine seated in the club-room, cradling a whiskey in his hands, lost in thought. I asked his permission to join him and sat down heavily.

"Mr. Purslaine, I want to offer my deepest apo—" I began, but he extended an admonitory hand.

"You have nothing to apologize for, Mr. Dalrymple. You warned us of the risks, and your Engine has performed beyond our expectations. Not a single subject has had a word of complaint about your performance."

"You are very kind. Nonetheless—"

Purslaine hushed me again. "Nonetheless, I am calling a halt to the experiment. You have honoured your side of our bargain, and the Brotherhood shall honour its. Our facilities and our resources are at your disposal for whatever your further project is, and you are our honoured guest for so long as you choose to remain with us."

"Thank you very much, Mr. President," I said quietly.

"I ask you only, and not in my official capacity, but as a personal favour, that you ensure that your infernal device go with you when you leave this place."

"It shall be so, sir," I said.

"Good. Leave me now. I wish to be alone with my thoughts."

Many members of the club, who had hitherto been so warm to me, displayed a certain discomfort in my presence now. Oliphant treated me as a long-lost brother, showing an ebullience that was impervious and uncongenial to my own sombre mood. Weaver and Dunlap were solid, sympathetic friends, assisting me in my labours and reminding me to rest when I became too caught up in the work. Inside of a fortnight, the Ontoscaphe was nearing completion.

Where the original craft had been fully enclosed, in a design reminiscent of a diving bell, the Ontoscaphe Mark II more nearly resembled a toboggan, low and open at the top, the better to be disassembled and transported back to ————shire.

"Now you return to your own home?" Weaver asked me one evening, as we were doing a final test of the connections on the 'scaphe.

"Impossible," I explained to him. "If I set out from this spot, I'd never find my way back to precisely my own ontosphere through all the vast realms of the Ontocycle. Only in the spot in which we arrived do I have any chance of detecting the trail that brought us hither and following it back. And that chance is more slender than I care to give much thought to. Further, there's no returning without Dewey."

"How do you plan to recover him from the Ministry?"

"I haven't the faintest notion. I need to make my way back to ——————shire and see what I can learn of his current whereabouts."

"It is a hazardous proposition."

"Indeed, but I see no choice."

Once we had contented ourselves that the Ontoscaphe was in as good a working order as could be ascertained without actually activating its functions, we disassembled it and packed the components into several massive steamer trunks for transport to ——————shire. Upon the completion of that, Dunlap and I shook hands warmly, and then he surprised me with a passionate kiss. "If ever you should find yourself in this ontosphere, in Manchester, once more, your assistance with the Tantalizer will always be most welcome," he said, and his eyes sparkled.

"Should that ever happen, I promise you that you shall have my aid for that project."

I looked for Weaver to thank him for all the aid and comfort he had given me over the previous month, but, failing to find him, I left him a long note, and retired, exhausted, to bed.

I slept better that night than I have in some time, and woke, tolerably refreshed, at dawn. I had arranged a cab to take me to the train station, but as I was unloading my trunks there, Weaver was suddenly at my side, assisting me with the heaviest of them. When we had pulled them to the kerb, he reached into a pocket and extracted two locomotive tickets. "I took the liberty of purchasing these," he told me, "since you were so slow about getting here."

I stared at them, silent.

"Well, you can't expect to go up against the whole bl—dy M of E unassisted! And I happen to know that you are an extremely diverting travelling companion. So that's settled."

"'Thank you, Alex," I said, tears standing out in my eyes.

"Oh, you'll be paying for my services," he chuckled. "I got us a private car."

"I shall endeavour to give satisfaction," I promised him.

Chapter 6: The Fugitive

As it transpired, an initial round, in which Weaver swallowed down my emission with characteristic gusto and I, in turn, brought him to several violent climaxes with my mouth upon his clitoris and my po-maded fingers stretching both his nether-holes, gave way rapidly to a discussion of strategy and tactics wherein we lit up cigars and debated our assault upon —————shire.

Weaver assured me that the Terminando would be long gone by this time, and any hunt for me would be thoroughly cursory. "Es-caped compulsories are two bob the dozen," he explained, "and most of them turn themselves in, in time. The term of service is neither more nor less than three years (with an annual three-week holiday), so all fugitives really do is prolong the disruption of their lives. The Ministry can afford to be patient—there's always more where they came from."

"But if that abominable Terminando is still wandering across the countryside, however are we to locate Dewey?"

"There's no telling if he's still with them or not, at any rate. A Ter-minando sends some conscripts back to regional centres to be de-ployed where they are needed and retains others for the duration, largely at the arbitor's discretion. In —————shire, we should at least be able to discover which was your friend's fate, and thus devise a plan of pursuit."

At the —————shire station, I went to hire a cab while Weaver remained with our trunks. When I returned to him, his face was ashen. I tried to ask him what was wrong, but he brushed off my questions and urged me to haste in loading the cab and making our way to the hotel.

Safely under way, he withdrew a folded handbill from his coat and passed it to me with a significant look. It read:

> WANTED
> BY THE MofEF
> NAME UNKNOWN, ALIAS: VICTOR DALRYMPLE
> HEIGHT: 6 FT; HAIR: LIGHT BROWN; EYES: BLUE; WEIGHT: APPROX. 14 STONE
> FOR DERELICITION OF COMPULSORY SERVICE; DE-STRUCTION OF MINISTRY PROPERTY; UNLICENSED OPER-ATION OF AN EROTOFLUIDIC DEVICE; HARMFUL TAMPERING WITH A COMPULSORY; AND IDENTITY FRAUD
> £100 REWARD

There was an engraving below.

"It's not a very good likeness," I said.

"I found it at the station," Weaver explained unnecessarily. "I rather doubt it was the only one printed up. One ton is a pretty sum of money..."

"Thinking of turning me in for the reward?" I asked, trying to lighten his anxious mood.

"Wondering why they're so keen to lay hands on you. Might your friend Dewey have revealed your secrets?"

"Impossible! Dewey would never intentionally betray us!"

"Have you ever felt the touch of a Motivator?"

"Not as such," I confessed.

"It does live up to its name remarkably well."

At the hotel, we found another handbill pinned to a tree out front, but there was little enough to be done about that. We checked in with-out incident and insisted in transporting our trunks ourselves, over the clerk's objections. He stared at us long and hard as we made our ways up and down the stairs, in a disconcerting way.

"I think he's recognized you," Weaver said when we were in our room.

"Then we haven't much time," I said. "Help me unpack."

Weaver looked quizzically at me. "If he is summoning the au-thorities, is settling into your room the best use for what time you have left of liberty?" he asked, as if reasoning with a small child.

"No," I told him briskly, "but a disguise might be."

"What good does a disguise do you if you've already been recog-nized?"

"That, my friend, depends on the quality of the disguise. Now hurry! We haven't much time."

Twenty minutes later, there was a sound of voices without. Weaver looked out the window and cursed quietly. "There's the little Judas now, leading a pair of Ministry Thuggis right here."

"I need more time!" I told him.

"I'd say you have three minutes. Maybe less."

"Then I suppose we must work with what we have. Be so kind as to don this circlet, please?"

"Victor, is this safe?"

"Not in the slightest. What an obtuse question."

"I should warn you that I'm not feeling terribly amorous at the moment."

"Understandable, but not necessarily problematic. With all the fail-safes removed, the amount of vital fluid needed for a transforma-tion should be relatively modest."

"How wonderfully reassuring. Are they really very likely to not notice a sabre-toothed parsnip or something? The results of the engine are not consistently inconspicuous."

"Your point is well taken, but what is likely is that they will not attempt to arrest one. If I become something excessively outré, simply hide me under the bed if I'm small enough. They will be looking for a man, not a root vegetable."

"And how long will the effects last?"

"I have no idea at all."

"Well then. Excelsior!"

We sat on the bed and listened to the men attempt, not very skilfully, to sneak down the corridor to our room. Weaver hummed the first few bars of "With Catlike Tread" from Pirates of Penzance, desisting only when I elbowed him sharply in the ribs. A key slid into the latch, and then the door was thrown open.

The two soldiers sprang into the room, drawing the ratty little clerk along with them like an autumn leaf behind a speeding locomotive. They looked at the two of us, then back at the clerk. "These are the violas who were accompanying the fugitive?" one of them asked.

"They—they—one of them was..." stammered the poor man, blinking rapidly at me.

"What is the meaning of this?" Weaver thundered, his five-foot-two frame managing to overshadow the taller soldiers as he crackled with magnificently feigned indignation. "How dare you barge into our room like this?"

"We received information that you may be harbouring the fugitive Victor Dalrymple," the man answered coolly.

"Is there room to hide this Dalrymple fellow in our room?" Weaver said, gesturing to encompass our rather modest accommodations. "Perhaps you'd like to check in the chamber pot, or under the night stand?"

"It—was her!" the clerk finally managed to squeak out, pointing to me. "Or him! Or her! That was Dalrymple! I'm sure of it."

The other lictor sighed and nodded. "Don't get a great many violas out this way, do you, old fellow? This—individual—here is not our man, or indeed any man at all, in the traditional sense of the term."

He patted the clerk's shoulder reassuringly. "It's an understandable error, so we shan't beat the tar out of you for wasting our time. But I'd urge you not to do it again, for the sake of your own health and welfare."

Then he turned to us. "Sorry to interrupt you... gentlemen," that last said with an ironical sneer. "We shan't be disturbing you again," he said, and the three of them filed out of the room, the clerk still sputtering his confusion and dismay.

Livid with indignation (genuine this time), Weaver made as if to follow him, but I caught his arm. "'Traditional sense of the term,'" he hissed between clenched teeth. "I'll show him the traditional sense of a good pummelling!"

"Low profile, old fellow." I urged him, grasping his shoulder. "We are trying to maintain a low profile."

"Very well," he said, "but only because more pressing matters present themselves."

"Indeed. The sooner we find out—"

"Getting a better look at you," he interrupted me. "Face me full on."

Blushing, I complied, and he ran his eyes over me so intently, his gaze seemed nearly palpable. "I do believe you may have managed to improve upon the original," he said at last. "That magnificent bosom is—"

"Heavy? Inconvenient? Ill-suited to my clothes?" I interrupted.

"—irresistible," he said, closing the difference between us. Though diminished in stature, I still had several inches on my diminutive friend, who locked his gaze with mine as the back of his knuckles slid lightly over my chest, which now strained so tightly against my waistcoat.

The sensation was electric. As you well recall, my dear, my nipples have always been a favourite source of pleasurable sensation for me, but this was far beyond any such I have ever felt. I gasped, and Weaver grinned.

He set to unfastening my buttons as rapidly as he could, but I protested: "We have no time to waste! There are matters we must investigate at once!"

"Indeed there are," he murmured distractedly, without pausing his operations upon my buttons.

When my waistcoat was open, he tugged my shirt up to my chin at once, and seized my breasts in his small, greedy hands. I let out a small noise at the sensation of skin against skin. Then his mouth found one broad pink nipple, and I confess I do not recall the events of the next several seconds.

The next moment I recall, I was on my back on the bed, pressing Weaver's head to my breast, where he sucked and licked voraciously. There was a swollen sensation within my trousers like and yet unlike that of a familiar cock-stand. A moment later, his fingertips brushed my groin, and I cried out aloud.

"Hush," Weaver urged me, and kissed me on the lips, his mouth hot and demanding, shoving mine open even as his nimble fingers unfastened my trousers.

As he tugged them down, I was for a moment seized by the fear that he might reveal some exotic amalgam like Oliphant's, but Weaver's hungry eyes showed no surprise at the sight that met them, only pleasure.

His fingers explored, sending ripples of exquisite sensation up through my belly, then one fierce jolt of sensation, almost too much to be borne. I choked back a cry. "That would be my clitoris, then," I gasped out.

"Indeed it would," Weaver agreed. "Here, perhaps I should be employing more delicate instruments of exploration for this task."

With remarkable agility, he was off the bed, kneeling, with my bottom perched at the very edge, urging my splayed legs upward over the bed. Then his face was buried between my legs, his lively brown eyes still watching my face as his tongue explored my cleft.

He showed a care and forbearance I had not often seen in him, stimulating my nether-parts with great delicacy, so that I was whimpering and squirming, attempting to gain more sensation from his teasing tongue before I felt it strum against my clitoris a second time. Once fastened, though, he was relentless, maintaining his implacable rhythm even while I pounded at the mattress, gnawed at my hands, and finally stiffened into the convulsions of climax.

He slowed for a time, his eyes sparkling with mischief as he resisted my attempts to push his face away from its secure berth, but shortly he was driving me up to the precipice once more, bringing me to a second peak in little more time than it now takes me to write it.

Only after that second orgasm did he relent sufficiently to stand and actually remove my poor abused travelling-suit before moving on to his own clothes, which joined mine in a confused mound on the hotel room's floor.

He rejoined me on the bed, his soft little bosom against my larger, firmer one, his legs twined with mine to bring our mottes together in the traditional attitude of the tribade.

"Never in my life have I really wished for a flesh cock," he murmured to me, "but just now I do wish I could spend inside that sweet little fanny of yours."

"Wouldn't that be just the thing?" I said. "To return home not just transfigured, but *enceinte* to boot."

"That might potentially be awkward," Weaver conceded. "I suppose we'd best stick to frigging for the time being." Which saying, he sucked for a moment at two of his fingers, then pressed them against my tender labia.

"Oh," I said, as I apprehended his intention. "I'm not certain that I—"

But Weaver interrupted me with his mouth on mine. Down below, I felt the pressure of his fingers grow, and grow, and then!

Oh!

They were pressed within me, stretching me most deliciously. He held them there for a time, allowing me to grow accustomed to the sensation.

"No maidenhead?" he asked with an ironical grin.

"I am not... quite... so innocent as I appear, sir," I gasped out, before his mouth found my bosom once more, and speech became impossible for both of us.

I think it was my fifth climax after which I managed to muster a demand for a break with sufficient authority to check Weaver's enthusiasm.

"There is the danger of me changing back at any moment," I told him as we pulled our clothes back on. "But on the other hand, it could also be weeks or months, so I don't see much worth in simply lurking about here until it occurs. We'd best do what we can to gather information about the Terminando with as much dispatch as possible."

"Let us hie ourselves to the local publicans, therefore, and see what the populace can reveal to us."

"Curious how your plans always hinge upon going drinking."

"Slander! Fully half my plans involve venery instead."

"Or in addition."

"Or in addition."

The Scarlet Drake was having a quiet afternoon. A labourer was working his way, with more diligence than table manners, through a massive kidney pie and what appeared to be his fourth glass of porter. Two old farmers in the corner were arguing in low tones over glasses of whiskey they never seemed to actually drink from. A half-dozen young men in erotofluidic livery clustered at one table, conversing quietly. We averted our eyes from this party, hoping to avoid notice. We took seats at the bar and ordered shandies from a barmaid who appeared to be in imminent danger of expiring from surfeit of ennui even as she poured us our drinks.

We nursed our pints, waiting for the Ministry men to leave, but they showed no haste to do so, their conversation becoming more boisterous, then falling to curious hush. A few minutes later, I heard one of them approaching us, his hesitant steps suggesting that he had been urged to do so by his fellows. "Pardon me, gentlemen," he said over my shoulder, showing only the slightest pause before the term. "May I, er, stand you a round of drinks?"

I looked around at him, and my jaw fell open in amazement. He recoiled at my stricken expression, and he and Weaver spoke at once.

"I am very sorry if I gave offence!" the technologist cried. "I did not mean—!"

"Thank you, but we would prefer to—" Weaver said.

But I recovered myself, and interrupted them both. "Thank you very much," I said. "Please do join us."

The technologist let out a considerable breath of relief and perched himself on the stool next to mine, Weaver looking quizzically at me.

"Pardon my intrusion," the technologist stammered. "One doesn't see so many violas out here in —————shire, as a rule, and you fellows are so... so...." He flushed.

Weaver nodded slowly and smiled indulgently. "You fancy us!"

Our interlocutor blushed still further at this, and I realized that Weaver had indeed "hit the nail upon the head," as the saying goes. I decided to take the reins of the conversation before this awkward seduction proceeded any further.

"I am Edwin Worchester, and this is my friend Alex Weaver," I said, extending my hand.

He took it. "It is a great pleasure. I am—"

"Dewey Panopea," I said, and his eyes widened. I continued more softly: "Late of Tesla Hall."

He stared at me for a long moment, then pursed his lip to form the initial V of my name. "Edwin," I prompted him, acutely aware that his fellow-troupers were still behind us, no doubt closely tracking the progress of Dewey's attempt at seduction.

"Edwin," he breathed. "You are... translated!"

"And yet which of us has made an ass of himself?" I retorted.

"I've been so—" he began, but I interrupted him once more.

"It is quite a pleasure to meet you, Mr. Panopea," I said loudly, "and I would be delighted to enlarge our acquaintance later this evening. Perhaps you would be interested in dropping by our hotel room for more conversation."

"That... sounds most enjoyable," he answered.

"Excellent." In a quieter tone, I told him the address at which we were staying, and then indicated that the interview was at a close. When he returned to his party, there was much cheering and back-clapping, as drinks were pressed into both his hands. Weaver and I hurriedly finished our drinks and exited the establishment.

"That was your friend?" Weaver whispered as we made our way up the path.

"It was."

"I thought you said he'd been conscripted!"

"That had certainly been my own impression. But Dewey does have a remarkable knack for landing on his feet."

"Well! He appears to have been... er... promoted. This does rather simplify matters, what?"

"Does it? I certainly hope so."

Dewey knocked softly on the door of our room at the appointed hour, and we let him in.

"Victor, whatever happened to—" Then he interrupted himself: "No, that's a stupid question. You built an engine."

"Very astute," I conceded.

He looked me up and down. "It suits you!"

"You are too kind," I said with ill grace. "You seem to have done rather well yourself. The long arm of the law rests surprisingly easy 'pon your shoulders."

He beamed. "Yes, this erotofluidic business is quite the lark, is it not?"

"Is it?"

"Well, if you're an eleven, it is. Apparently, I'm only the third they've ever found. Once they established that, they treated me like I was made of blown glass. And now that—"

"Hold, hold, hold!" I said. "This is all quite too much! What is it that happened, in order, since I last saw you?"

"Very well, I'll tell you the whole story," Dewey said, claiming the room's sole easy chair, and leaning back comfortably. "But I warn you, it isn't short."

"I didn't think it would be," I said.

Chapter 7: The Compulsory

"Well," Dewey told me, "I was tempted to change forms and make my escape after the explosion, but really there was no hurry. I could fly off any time I liked, so it seemed wiser to remain in place for the time being and keep the Terminando's hands full while you made your own escape.

"When Davis made it back to the station, the arbitor was quite livid to learn you had escaped. And when she learned that Mrs. Wigglesworth was incapacitated (which she of course blamed on you), she got a curious look in her eyes, and said, 'Two problems; one solution' in a rather frightening tone of voice. Half an hour later, the Terminando was packed up, and Davis, quite nude except for the bit shoved in his mouth to stifle his cries, was shackled on the front of the *Albion*, his bottomhole distended with the stimulator."

"Mrs. Wigglesworth?" I asked.

"Oh, the arbitor called her Dimples. She had the habit of devising the most dreadful pet names for all the compulsories she recruited. I was Crumpet."

I winced.

"So they wired back to headquarters about my case and broke camp, and we made our way towards Congleton.

"I was exempt from engine service, since Hodgkins was concerned that my output would overload the machinery once more, so it was rather a tedious journey for me. I was kept shackled inside the *Albion*, allowed only the most wholesome and improving modern novels to read.

"In Congleton, however, things got livelier. A special erotometer had been brought in. When I showed some curiosity about its workings, Hodgkins rather warmed to me for the first time, explaining with awe that 'it goes to eleven.' I suggested a few points for improvement, based on Uncle Daedalus's special devices for working with Eleanor, which led to a long, whispered consultation between the technologist and the arbitor.

"I confess, to my mortification, that that arbitor truly had the measure of me. I was strapped into the equipment once more, and she stripped herself to her small-clothes, showing quite well-turned calves, the better to don a massive ivory godemiche, intricately carved with scenes from the Battle of Trafalgar. She moved with an unhurried deliberation more sinister than any more deliberate menacing could possibly be, and by the time she stepped towards me, I was already flushed and trembling with anticipation of the ordeal in store for me.

"She lifted my chin with one slender fingertip, forcing me to meet her gaze, so that I might glimpse the heat smouldering beneath her external cool. At that moment, I knew that I was before a predator as perfectly adapted to her environment as the Bengal tiger or the great white shark.

"Her finger trailed down my torso, until her hand rested just above my navel.

"'It is,' she purred to me, 'our great good fortune that the Compulsory Service regulations were written by a group of singularly stupid and unresourceful men. I am enjoined most strictly from taking this handsome cock of yours in my cunny, because, were that to be permitted, I might be tempted to do so for selfish reasons, rather than to discipline you or to promote the generation of erotofluidic force.'

"My unruly prick, as if recognizing its name, was rising to meet her steady hand. Vainly, I gritted my teeth and clenched my fists, attempting to forestall the moment when the two would touch.

"She continued speaking: 'No such constraints, however, bar me from strapping on this daunting artefact of the scrimshander's craft, and buggering you quite senseless.'

"At that phrase, my cock rose the final millimetre, and her hand closed upon it with the rapidity of a Venus fly-trap.

"'...a course of action to which, I tell you in the strictest confidence, I am rather more disposed in the first place,' she finished.

"I can still barely speak of the dreadful ordeal that followed. It was a tour-de-force of the arbitor's art. She was as good as her word with the ivory dildoe, taking me in a variety of inventive attitudes, her cunning fingers playing up and down my body, teasing my cock again and again to the brink of climax before denying me the final release.

"Her tongue was everywhere, lapping up my perspiration, my pre-ejaculatory fluid, and my helpless tears with equal gusto.

"At long last, one of her hands disappeared within her drawers. She sighed—a long, shuddering noise—then the hand reappeared, shining wet. She held it beneath my nose and ordered me to inhale, while her other hand maintained a fierce grip on my purple member. The godemiche was lodged to the hilt in my bottom-hole, and she rocked her hips minutely against mine so that its apex moved deep within me. The aroma of that cruel woman's excitement inflamed my brain, and I howled in subjugation, firing my spunk up over my own head to strike the enhanced erotometer, where it popped and sizzled like water upon a hot skillet.

"After a long pause, the arbitor slowly removed the many long inches of her godemiche from my bottom-hole, then kissed me warmly on the mouth, the first and only time she has granted me such an intimacy.

"She stood, and grinned at her gathered minions. 'I almost feel that I should submit my letter of resignation to the Ministry today,' she said. 'I doubt that my future holds a finer performance than you just witnessed. Hodgkins?'

"'Eleven point three,' Hodkgins reported. 'And I'd junk this 'meter were I you, Arbitor. It's half-fried at this point. And not the cleanest.'

"Ignoring her assistant's advice, she turned to the lictors. 'See to the compulsory,' she directed them. 'Be gentle with him—he's had rather a trying day. Knock me up in an hour, when I've had time to... refresh myself.'"

∾

"My goodness," Weaver ejaculated. "What a gripping narrative! I feel quite breathless just listening to it."

I grinned. Dewey's charms were considerable, and it was no surprise to see my violan friend succumbing to them. I stood.

"Storytelling is thirsty work," I said. "Perhaps I should see about acquiring us some refreshments."

"Capital idea!" said Weaver with a bit too much enthusiasm. "Just the thing."

I sauntered down to the front desk, where the clerk from the day before glared at me suspiciously. I requested a bottle of sherry and three glasses, then stood, humming to myself, while he clanked about in the kitchen for a time.

I returned to find Dewey standing in a corner of the room. Weaver stood before him, barely failing to touch, his hands pressed against the walls on Dewey's either side, forming a cage in which my Geoduck friend flushed and squirmed with more alarm than displeasure. Murmuring soothing words, Weaver took hold of Dewey's chin, and leaned his face in.

I cleared my throat, and Dewey started, instantly extricating himself from Weaver's attentions. "Victor! You're back!" he said.

"I am," I said.

"Shall I, erm, resume my tale?"

"I think you'd best finish it before we move on to other activities," I said.

Weaver favoured me with a resentful glare as he re-seated himself, one which I affected not to notice.

∾

"Well," Dewey said. "The roads outside Congleton were particularly abominable, and despite the arbitor's skilful driving, and despite Hodgkins's best efforts at maintenance (he was really an erotofluidicist by training, not a mechanic), break-downs became an all-too-regular feature of our travels. One day, after a mechanical break-down,

Hodgkins was underneath the *Albion*, cursing steadily in a low voice as he endeavoured to effect a repair. His difficulties in finding the problem arose primarily from his being in entirely the wrong area of the engine, a point which I attempted to raise, as tactfully as I could. He turned and stared at me for a long moment, shackled as I was, nude, to the craft. 'Well, if you're so bl—dy clever, why don't you fix it yourself?' he said, though his tone showed less rancour than the words might lead one to expect.

"Now it was my turn to stare silently.

"'You think you could?' he said at last.

"'I'd be happy to try,' I said, more from boredom than pride.

"'And you won't give me no trouble?' he asked, little aware that I could make my exit any time I took a liking to.

"'I shall be as meek as the proverbial lamb.'

"With considerable grumbling, he found the appropriate keys and unshackled me, whereupon I crawled 'neath the craft and had repaired the connection in something rather less than a quarter of an hour, at which time I returned to my prior spot and allowed Hodgkins to reattach me to the engine.

"When another problem arose that day, Hodgkins went so far as to solicit my advice, and when the arbitor returned from her constitutional, she found the two of us working together to loosen a particularly stubborn pipe. 'Hodgkins,' she said, with some asperity, 'what are you doing with the compulsory?'

"Hodgkins flushed to his collar. 'I'm very sorry, Arbitor,' he stammered. 'He is really very good with engines, and we are in a hurry.'

"'Ministry regulations forbid employing compulsories for manual labour,' she said.

"'Yes, Arbitor. I'm sorry, Arbitor,' Hodgkins said.

"Then she leaned in and spoke more softly. 'But needs must when the Devil drives, and if he isn't behind these roads, I don't know who is. If this fellow wants to blacken his pretty little hands, you need to at least throw a uniform on him, for appearance's sake. Am I understood?'

"Hodgkins nodded frantically. 'Certainly, Arbitor! I promise!'

"She smiled coolly. 'Very good.'

∾

"So that was that, then! After each repair, Hodgkins would request the return of his spare uniform with the most poignant look of guilt upon his face, as if spending the day naked and shackled were some sort of hardship.

"In time, nudity became something like a dress uniform for me. I worked and ate with the rest of the *Albion*'s crew as something between a peer and a mascot when crossing the countryside, and was stripped and shackled only for the Terminandos, squirming alongside Dimples and Bubbles. Even then I was not actually hooked up to the engine, which was far too fragile for my level-eleven output, though the arbitor would occasionally set me to gamahuching-duty for one of the other two compulsories, positioning me between the women's thighs to lick and suck in heat and darkness for hours, enjoined with the direst threats to avert inducing orgasm—a duty I found profoundly gratifying.

"Then, some weeks in, we arrived in one small town to find an urgent wire awaiting us, directing all local Ministry personnel to hasten to ————shire at once.

"Hesitantly, Porter said, 'What's the emergency, Arbitor?'

"'I do not know,' she said simply.

"'Isn't ————shire where we picked up Dewey?'

"'Indeed. And where we... misplaced... his interesting friend.'

"Her reference to your escape cowed Davis and Porter enough that they performed the rest of the packing-up in perfect silence, well aware that their failure had cost them dearly in their superior's esteem.

"An hour's travel out from ————shire, the arbitor called out, 'Hodgkins, make Crumpet presentable,' and he sprang to fetch the shackles.

"But before I could undress, there came a shout from ahead upon the road: "'Hold your place and name your business!'

"Four men in Ministry uniforms, armed with motivators and pistol-belts, stood blocking our way.

"She brought the *Albion* to an abrupt halt that nearly sent Hodgkins and me crashing to the floor. 'The ipsekinetron *Albion*,' she answered crisply.

"One of them men looked us over, scribbling in a memorandum book. 'One arbitor," he said, half to himself, "two lictors, two compulsories, two technologists.' Then he looked up. 'Correct?'

"The arbitor was silent for one beat. 'Just so.'

"There was a yowl from Dimples as the *Albion* shuddered to life once more, and we proceeded down the road. I looked at Hodgkins. Hodgkins was looking at me. 'Welcome to the corps,' he said, suppressing a smile.

☙

"————shire, as you have seen, was crawling with every rank of Ministry worker by the time we arrived, hastily constructed barracks already housing the hundred or so technologists and lictors who were busily erecting fences, digging ditches, and generally transforming the sleepy town into a positive beehive of bureaucratic and para-military diligence, extending as far into the countryside as the meadow in which we arrived.

"I have been living in the technologists' barracks, helping to maintain the machinery that powers and lights the complex. The other engineers have been splendid fellows, by and large, and I've learned an amazing amount about erotofluidics, but I must say it's rather a relief to have you finally show up.

"When I was with the Terminando, the arbitor always seemed to rather make a point of ensuring that I have a good spend every day or so. I think the loss of all that equipment back in ————shire made a bit of an impression, and they were anxious not to see me too pent up.

"Once I was trying to pass for a technologist, though, life became considerably more dreary. What with the amount of work they've been throwing at us, and my efforts to keep a low profile, I've barely been getting any attention at all!

"After my first three days here, I was positively bursting at the seams. The barracks didn't allow me any privacy, and I knew practically no one.

"I was sent to the central power station, which, judging by the good-natured teasing from the other technologists, was considered a bit of a plum assignment.

"The station appeared to be a former mill building. When I entered through a low tin door, the smells and sounds of erotofluidic generation struck me with exceptional force. Fully a dozen identical collection machines were arrayed across the room, each supporting a nude figure which bucked in an advanced state of amorous excitement. Over the faint whir of machinery, the cries of the compulsories and the buzz and crackle of powerful erotofluidic forces mingled in counterpoint; the smell mingled machine oil, ozone, sweat, and the fluids of male and female excitement in an overpowering cocktail.

"Station number seven was my destination, and the junior arbitor on guard there introduced himself as Bert and rose from his stool to show me the situation.

"'These new-style collection machines, with the Dunlap regulators, practically run themselves,' he explained. 'Why, a monkey could do my job at this point.'

"He moved his attention from the machinery to the subject who moaned and squirmed atop it. 'This 'ere's Lady FitzHugh her own self, if ye can believe that,' he said, laying one hand familiarly on the compulsory's heaving flank, 'only three months into her term of service.'

"I watched, transfixed, as Her Ladyship twisted and writhed against the Vibratorium, tendrils of chestnut hair clinging to her flushed forehead, gulping for breath around the gag that distorted her mouth as she struggled to obtain the climax that just eluded her.

"The buzzing of the Vibratorium came to an abrupt stop, and Her Ladyship wailed in despair, continuing to thrust her hips quite obscenely against the now-inert pad of the Vibratorium. Her eyes, wide and beseeching, turned to the arbitor who had deactivated the device.

"'She... she seems to be performing quite adequately,' I ventured, mesmerized by the lovely woman's ardent struggles.

"'Oh, 'er ladyship is a gem indeed,' he agreed. 'A full eight on 'er good days, an' that's the honest truth. No, station number seven is our problem 'ere. The power output's all funny—there's a loose connection somewhere. Think ye can find it?'

"'I'll try,' I said, and then set to work. The collection station was a well-built piece of equipment, easy to comprehend and maintain. Were it not for the intensely distracting sights and sounds all around me, I could probably have located the problem in five minutes. With the vulnerable, ardent body bucking a scant foot from my hands, and the similar sights in all directions, it took me almost half an hour to locate and correct the problem. That finished, I gathered up my tools and stood gaping, my cock painfully hard, as it had been nearly since arriving in the power station.

"'Yer new here, ain't ya?' the arbitor behind me said, and it took me a moment to realize I was the one addressed, so deep was the reverie that the sight of Lady FitzHugh's torment had induced in me.

"I started, certain that my imposture had been discovered and that I was about to be strapped to station number seven in place of Her Ladyship.

"Bert, however, continued imperturbably. 'Ye know the rules. No fuckin' 'em,' he said, then chuckled at my crestfallen expression. 'You can feel 'er up and wank yerself off if ye like, though.' He pulled a lever, and the device against Lady FitzHugh's mons retracted.

"Unable to believe my good fortune, I approached Her Ladyship, uneasy in my mind, but more aroused then ever. My hands moved to the flies of my painfully distended trousers and paused. My companion had sat down on his stool and extracted a periodical from a back pocket, which he flipped through idly. 'Take yer time,' he said, without looking up. 'I'm on the clock, and in no hurry.'

"The arrangement was far from ideal, but, in my current straits, irresistible. I extracted my furiously aroused cock, and with the other reached out and ran my fingers across the skin of Her Ladyship's belly.

"Any trepidation I might have harboured about her reluctance to participate in such proceedings were at once dispelled as she groaned and thrust her hips up towards me in unspeakably obscene invitation. My index finger traced along the delicate line of fuzz that ran from below her navel to the broad patch of dark curls between her legs.

"The finger ran over the crease of her thigh, teasing both her and myself, as my other hand began slowly pumping at my rigid member. Her hips worked from side to side, striving to capture more sensation from my fingertips.

"Her labia were engorged to a nearly-crimson hue, and glistening with moisture. To press a fingertip against them was to be drawn within at once, until the knuckle was against her mons, the remarkable heat and slickness of her noble vagina enclosing my finger.

"Her Ladyship's expression was unmistakable. 'More,' it demanded with an eloquence beyond mere words. Obligingly, two, then three, then four fingers pressed inside her in less time than it takes to say. A long shuddering wail was the noblewoman's reply. My other hand was rapidly becoming slick with my own emissions as my moisture answered hers.

"I slowed the motions on my cock, reluctant to bring on my climax too soon. The jerks of Her Ladyship's hips suggested that her nether-mouth yet hungered for further penetration, though her spasmodic contractions upon my knuckles were already nearly painful in their force.

"My thumb joined the other digits, first sliding along her opening to gather the necessary moisture, then working within, my hand rolled into as small a circumference as possible, then pressing inward in a series of patient thrusts, each apparent sticking-point giving way within moments, until only the merest crease between my palm and the heel of my thumb was visible, my fingertips pressed against the firm bulge of her cervix as she yet strove with her hips to take more of my hand within herself.

"My fingers, as if of their own accord, curled back, enclosing my thumb, and in a moment, the thickest part of my hand was past the band of muscle at the mouth of her cunt. Her Ladyship's pale blue eyes bulged wide, and a wild cry escaped her throat. The effect of her cunt's compression now reversed itself, drawing my fist further within, rather than pressing it outward. I was in her to the very wrist now, as her bottom continued to beat a tattoo upon the bench, demanding further penetration.

"The moist sounds generated by my hand moving in and out of

her excited orifice were echoed by the noise of my other hand upon my wildly excited member.

"Lady FitzHugh's bound heels planted themselves upon the bench, and her bottom rose slowly from its support, supporting herself solely on heels and shoulders, as her eyes pressed shut, her brow furrowing as her crisis clearly approached. The sharp cries that had previously been audible from behind her gag now gave way to a sustained wail, interrupted only briefly for great gasping breaths.

"'Good show, gov'ner,' the arbitor announced behind me. 'Bring 'er off now.'

"His advice distracted me only for an instant, and Her Ladyship not at all.

"A moment later, I cried out in pleasure. Lady FitzHugh's eyes snapped open just in time to focus upon my rigid member as it pulsed and fired a stream of semen across her ample bosom.

"As the hot fluid struck her, her own climax struck, and her vagina clamped down upon my hand with unprecedented force, nearly squeezing me out of her as she sprayed me quite to the elbow with her own clear emission.

"Both my hands kept at their parallel labours, the left riding out the last of Lady FitzHugh's contractions, the right coaxing subsequent spurts out of my own cock onto her belly, her hip, and finally a few thin drops onto the carpet at my feet.

"At last I removed my hand and took the bold liberty of leaning down and kissing Her Ladyship upon her lips, yet distorted with the gag, a gesture which she did not, under the circumstances, appear to consider impertinent, returning the kiss as much as her confinement allowed.

"Becoming aware of my surroundings once more, I looked around and saw that the arbitor was still engrossed in his penny dreadful. Feeling my gaze upon him, he glanced up. 'Don't look at me, gov,' he said. 'Ye can clean up yer own d———d mess.'"

Chapter 8: The Trebuchet

"What an abominable philistine!" Weaver exclaimed. "He should have offered to let you spunk in his mouth."

Dewey blushed. "Well, I mean, he was on duty, it isn't—"

"I certainly would have," Weaver put in, laying a hand gently on Dewey's knee. "In fact, I would be—"

"Very interested," I interrupted, "in hearing the rest of your story. Isn't that right, Weaver?"

Weaver shot me a look of irritation, but nodded.

Dewey, however, appeared to be well thrown off his stride. "Well... that's the gist of it. I've been maintaining the machinery and getting to know my fellows in the technologist corps. Today we had the afternoon off, so we went round to the pub for a few drinks."

"But what is going on here in ————shire?" I demanded. "What is the extraordinary event that has summoned all these personnel—is it somehow connected with us?"

"There are rumours, of course," Dewey said, "and the arbitors must know something. But nobody in the barracks has anything but guesses really. There's all sorts of strange projects being started and abandoned all over the place, as if the Ministry knows it needs to do something, but doesn't know what."

"Well, doesn't that narrow it down wonderfully," I said bitterly.

"I'm sorry," Dewey said, his voice sorrow itself, and Weaver leaned in to stroke his hand soothingly and tell him that that was quite all right, and nobody thought any the worse of him for it.

As they verbally danced about each other once more, I took the opportunity to assess our situation. The Ministry's crisis, whatsoever it might be, was certainly a considerable inconvenience, and even a threat, but not necessarily our concern directly. If we could find our way into the field in which we had arrived and assemble the Mark II, we could make our way home and leave this world to its strange troubles.

I voiced this thought to my companions, and Dewey's face was, if possible, even more crestfallen than before. "That may offer some challenges," he said. "I think you'd better have a look at the field."

∽

The three of us arrived just as the sun was starting to set, a great red disk casting into stark silhouette the hastily erected high wood walls and guard towers that surrounded what had been a vacant meadow a few weeks before.

After a silence, I spoke: "Well, that is most unexpected."

"And laborious, I must tell you," Dewey added brightly. "The poor carpenters were quite..." he saw my expression and trailed off. I did not have a great deal of empathy to spare for the Ministry of Erotofluidics' carpentry corps at that moment.

Escape, a resolution to my troubles, your own welcoming arms, the happy gurgles of little Margaret and Beatrice, all of which had seemed within reach an hour ago, for the first time in many weeks, now seemed as distant as ever.

"I need a drink," I announced.

"The Scarlet Drake should still be open," Dewey suggested, so we trudged wearily back into town and selected a booth in the back of that establishment.

I brought a round of brandies from the bar but found that Dewey had buried his nose in a newspaper he had found somewhere. I sat and passed my companions their drinks.

"So our next—" I began, but Dewey waved me to silence, his eyes fixed on the newspaper before him.

"Hush!" he demanded, and leaned in closer to the text before him. "Page seven, page seven," he muttered, rapidly riffling the paper, only to fling it open and bury his nose in its pages once more. "Something is terribly wrong," he said at last in a strange, low tone.

"I should bl—dy well think so," I ejaculated. "I ran up and down the length of the country, at considerable risk to life and limb, in an effort to rescue you, and then I find you too interested in reading the paper to even make civilized public-house conversation with me."

"Look!" he said, and reversed the paper, pointing to one headline, the singularly uninformative STRANGE DOINGS IN _____SHIRE.

"Another drunken yeoman reported a rain of frogs or some such?" I speculated. "I'm amazed the papers are still printing such stuff."

Dewey glared at me fiercely. "Another drunken yeoman reported a clutch of ducklings hatched with naked, featureless necks," he said. "And bodies encased in clam shells."

"How curious!" Weaver said.

"Well, that is certainly an odd coincidence," I conceded.

"How so?" Weaver asked.

Dewey ignored Weaver's puzzlement. "Coincidence? What do you make of this?" He pointed to the accompanying engraving, which I studied for a moment.

"A piglet born with a singularly ugly human face?"

He turned the page to Weaver. "What do you make of this?"

Weaver peered at the picture for a long moment. "Looks rather like... er... Edwin," he said at last.

"Nonsense!" I ejaculated. "There's no resemblance at all. Why, look at those close-set little eyes, that ridiculous, protuberant chin, those great, massive ears!"

There was a silence.

"Edwin," Weaver said, in a soothing tone, "you are a more than usually handsome fellow, and this is as handsome an idiot man-pig as can be reasonably expected."

"The notion is absurd," I protested. "Are you suggesting that I committed some sort of outrage with a sow?"

Dewey rolled his eyes with exasperation. "No more than I've been out having my way with waterfowl," he said. "This is ontology gone terribly wrong, or I'm no ontological engineer."

"Do you believe that some mad scientist is roaming about the countryside with an engine, experimenting on livestock?"

"I don't know," Dewey said, then, more anxiously, "I don't know! But I feel it must all be connected. These strange births, the ministry presence..." He trailed off.

"...and your arrival here last month," Weaver filled in.

"Well, it is a great deal to ask of coincidence," he said.

A terrible surmise then struck me. "A resonance cascade," I said.

"A what?" Weaver said.

Dewey shook his head. "That's only possible if you try to create an ontological field where none was before."

I was still as death, but my heart was racing in my chest. "What if you were to introduce one from an entirely different ontosphere?"

∾

Our unfinished drinks still in our booth at the Drake, we fairly sprinted back to our room, a single light of dawning understanding in Dewey's and my eyes, Weaver chasing after us, pleading futilely for some sort of explanation.

At the front desk, I rang up the innkeeper and demanded a pot of strong coffee, a sheaf of blotting paper, ink, pens, and a copy of Granville's Ontological Incidence Tables, as recent as practicable, to be delivered to our rooms without delay.

Already in his nightshirt, the proprietor protested the lateness of the hour until I induced Weaver to lay a shilling on the table, which concluded the debate with its characteristic expeditiousness.

The hours that followed were, truth be told, not unpleasurable. The unique thrill of scientific breakthrough was upon us, as Dewey and I filled sheet after sheet with diagrams, equations, formulae, and calculations. It was only as rose began to tinge the eastern horizon that the numb horror of our conclusions began to overtake the wild excitement of their pursuit.

"We've been fools," I said, slumped on the floor.

"Mad, reckless fools," Dewey echoed, in a like attitude beside me.

Weaver was snoring softly upon the bed, having retreated there in frustration when we refused to spare him the effort to explain our work to him.

"This poor, poor world," I said, looking about me at the flocked wall-paper, the exquisite dawn outside the window, my friend the viola, still rather fetching with his mouth open and a small trail of saliva across one cheek.

"How long do you give it?" Dewey said.

"At this point? Perhaps another week. Perhaps a bit less."

"We'll be killed as well, of course," Dewey observed.

"It only seems proper, under the circumstances."

There was a groan from the bed. The morning sun had awakened Weaver, and he had lifted his head to survey the room, covered as it was in scattered papers, some crumpled and thrown into a corner, most covered densely with figures and diagrams.

"Have you... figured out what's going on?" he asked.

There was a moment's silence.

"I believe so," I said.

Something in my voice must have given him some inkling as to the gravity of the situation, as he sat bolt upright. "But?"

"But we're all going to die," said Dewey flatly.

"Sooner than had previously been thought?"

"This month," Dewey said. "Catastrophically."

"I realize that I asked," Weaver said peevishly, "but you really might encourage a fellow to have his first cup of tea before you inflict intelligence of that sort on him. Why, at this hour of the day, I might find that datum, presented thus, rather discouraging."

"I'm sorry," Dewey said. "I'm so, so sorry." And he put his face in his hands and began to sob.

In a flash, Weaver was off the bed and crouching beside Dewey, arm about the younger man's shoulders. "There, there, old fellow," he said gently, "There's no need for all that. I'm certain you and Victor can come up with a solution in time. Why, you fellows are couple of miracle workers, what? I mean, as old Victor tells it, no-one else had any idea other ontospheres even existed. And you lads managed to actually travel to one! Why, after that, you're not going to let a little obstacle like this stop you, are you?"

Weaver's words seemed to have a soothing effect on Dewey, who looked plaintively at him. "You... you really think there might be some way out?"

Weaver smiled warmly. "I am certain of it. Now let us go get some breakfast, and we can see if we can figure some way out of this little difficulty."

"A-all right," Dewey said.

Weaver kissed him warmly on the lips and pulled him to his feet.

∾

Weaver tore, with an unholy gusto, into a massive plate of eggs, beans, toast, and bacon while Dewey nibbled at some toast with marmalade and I attempted to cast our discoveries in layman's terms.

"You recall that line from Wordsworth, 'Trailing clouds of glory do we come'? It's rather like that, only for 'glory,' read 'catastrophically destructive ontological resonance cascades.'"

"Really does nothing for the scansion...." Weaver muttered with his mouth full.

"In a certain sense," I continued, ignoring his remark, "when we passed from our world into this, what we did was to erase our ontological fields there, and abruptly impose them onto this world. What we didn't realize is that when one does this, one runs a small chance of creating a sort of Charybdis, a run-away vortex of ontological force that feeds upon all the ontologies about it."

"So... more naked-headed ducks and Victor-headed piglets to come?"

"That's just the very faintest beginning," I said, gesturing so that I almost upset the marmalade pot. "The components of the vortex will be all disordered, and getting ever stronger. A piglet born with my face is a curiosity. A piglet born with Dewey's big toe in place of a head is stillborn. And any day now it won't be just foetuses. Living people and things will be transformed as well. Unless we made an error in our calculations, within a week, all living things in England will be transformed into a hodge-podge of parts of Dewey, me, and whatever skin and intestinal parasites we carried with us on the journey. Within a few hours of that, the entire Earth will have succumbed. A few days after that, whatever populations Mars and Venus possess will be similarly fatally transfigured. And outward from there, in every direction, throughout all Creation."

This, at last, had induced Weaver to pause in his ravenous consumption. "And there's no way to stop this?" he asked.

"None that we can see," I answered sadly.

He sopped up the last of his egg yolk with a corner of toast and stuffed it into his mouth. "Bl—dy h—l," he lisped around the morsel. He took a great gulp of tea. "Can it be contained somehow? Enclosed while it's still relatively small?"

I shook my head. "Organic matter will be transformed. Inorganic it will pass through like light through leaded glass."

"Explosives?"

"Won't touch it."

"The Engine?"

"Intriguing," I conceded. "But futile. The vortex in there has been building in strength and coherence for a month now. The chaotic ontological fields produced by the engine would just be absorbed as one more tiny particle of fuel."

He nodded pensively. "What about using the Mark II?"

"I won't claim it hasn't crossed my mind. But to flee now, after we've doomed this entire world... I may not be a good man, but I'm a better man than that. No, we stand and fight this, to the bitter end."

Dewey, who had been gazing sullenly into the dregs of his tea, looked up abruptly. "I don't think that's what he means, Victor."

I looked at him in confusion.

"Look, no other waveform can disturb the vortex, but the original waveform...." He trailed off into silence.

"Dewey, if you shoot a man through the chest, firing the same musketball through the wound in the other direction isn't going to cure him."

"That's a stupid analogy. If you drop a boulder on a man's foot, removing it does him more good than leaving it there."

"No, that's a stupid analogy!" I said. "Why, if you—" I realized that other diners were staring at me in some alarm. Then I realized that I had been shouting. "I apologize. It's been a long night."

"Victor," Weaver said gently, "I still haven't heard you say, with confidence, that it wouldn't work."

I poured myself some more tea, sweetened it, and stirred it. "I confess that I hadn't considered the notion," I said at last. "I was so caught up in the idea that using the 'scaphe was an act of cowardice that I hadn't thought of it as a solution."

"So you're not certain that it would be ineffectual."

"Well, no, but—"

"And if you don't do it?"

"We all die," Dewey volunteered. "Gruesomely."

"I'm no ontological engineer, but I confess that that sounds like a point in its favour," Weaver ventured.

"Perhaps."

Back at the room, we went back over our figures and diagrams. "If this is to work," I concluded, "the 'scaphe must be activated from within the vortex, ideally from the very spot where it arrived."

"All right," Weaver said.

"Not so fast. The effect of the vortex should be far less on Dewey and myself than on any other living matter, but that still gives us..." I did some quick arithmetic. "...some two-and-a-half to seven seconds between entering the vortex and complete ontological disintegration."

"That does rather present some difficulties." He massaged his forehead with two fingers. "So you would have to somehow fling the entire craft, passengers and all, into the midst of it."

I shook my head impatiently. "Using what?"

"A giant trebuchet?" Dewey said.

"A what?" I snapped.

"A trebuchet," Weaver put in. "It's a sort of siege engine, with a counterweight, and a great Archimedean—"

"Yes," I snapped irritably. "I know what it is, I'm a bl—dy engineer. If we happened to have brought along a giant trebuchet, that would do very nicely indeed."

The frustration of the night was taking its toll, and I continued to twist the knife, my voice dripping with bitter irony: "Oh blast! I neglected to bring mine along. Weaver, do you happen to have a giant trebuchet about your person?"

Weaver was silent.

"Dewey, do you have ready access to a giant trebuchet?"

"I might," he said.

"Well, then, since none of us is in possession of such a device, perhaps we should confine—Wait, what?"

"I spent some time with a ballistics engineer, in from London, last week. He had the most lovely big brown eyes, and a remarkable long, slender—"

"Trebuchet," I interrupted him curtly.

"Right! He mentioned to me that he couldn't imagine what the devil the Ministry wanted with a giant trebuchet. He asked if I knew of any medieval keeps in the neighbourhood that we intended to lay siege to."

"Dewey," I said, "I wish to apologize for casting aspersions upon your intelligence-gathering acumen previously. Truly, you have a rare gift for espionage."

Dewey blushed and stammered; then the sound of a party of Ministry staff caused him to glance at the window.

"I'm terribly late!" he announced. "I was supposed to be adjusting the lighting cables at eight!"

"The world is ending," I reminded him. "I think you may be permitted a holiday for the occasion."

"You just say that because you haven't met Arbitor Sterling," he protested. "Why, once she—Oh, I'd best tell you at lunch break. I'll be by then to see how you fellows are getting on."

Dewey ran out of the room, leaving Weaver and myself alone. "Very well," I said, "We shall have to do what we can to gather information in the meantime." I sat down on the bed; my head felt extremely heavy. I decided it could do no harm to recline for a moment. "The first order of business will be to figure out whether..."

Weaver later told me that I actually managed to fall asleep mid-sentence.

I awoke with a start when Dewey entered the room. There was a horrid taste in my mouth, the sun was high in the sky, and Weaver was nowhere to be seen.

"Not to worry," Dewey announced. "I have found the perfect solution."

"Oh?" I said, attempting to clear the sleep out of my eyes.

"I explained the whole matter to our arbitor, Miss Gibson. She of course responded that she would be ever so interested in clearing up all our little difficulties."

"The one who first arrested us? Are you mad?"

"Now, I realize that I should perhaps have consulted with you fellows first, but I just knew that she is precisely the person to help us out. Such a wise, dignified woman! She rather reminds me of Daedalus."

"You mean arrogant, blinkered, and temperamental?"

Dewey coloured a bit. "You shouldn't say such things! Even in jest!"

"Who was jesting?"

"At any rate, she said she'd hurry over at once; she was particularly eager to see you again."

"Oh, I can just imagine!" I said, looking wildly about the room. There was only one door. I leaned my head out the window. Two floors below me, a set of cucumber-frames presented a distinctly unappealing landing site.

I pulled my head back inside and made for the door. "Victor Dalrymple," came a familiar cool, female voice. I nearly had apoplexy as I registered a slender figure in brown livery seated on the room's bed.

My heart was still hammering in my chest as I resolved to make a brave face of it. "Who?" I gasped.

"Victor Dalrymple," Gibson repeated. "Fugitive, thief, vandal," she recited the list with some relish, "operator of an unlicensed erotofluidic device... and foreign agent!"

I bristled. "I say! I am an Englishman and a patriot!"

"From an entirely different world."

To this I gave no reply.

"An extremely foreign agent," she amplified.

"If I am such a threat, why don't I see your bully boys here?" I said, sternly reminding myself that the effects of the Engine upon me had rendered the traditional prohibitions against striking a woman rather less binding upon my person.

She stood, and suddenly a motivator was gleaming in her hand, its faint buzz distinctly audible in the room's quiet. "You think I need them to control you? You are mistaken."

I assumed a Queensbury fighting stance and prepared for altercation.

Dewey was off to one side, waving his arms and shouting about unfortunate misunderstandings and terrible mistakes and no need for alarm.

In my peripheral vision, the door was flung open, but I kept my eyes fixed on my opponent. She did likewise, still edging towards me with the motivator at the ready.

"Excellent news!" came Weaver's voice from the hallway. "The Brotherhood is sending its—" His voice trailed off as he took in the tableau before him. Then, uncertainly, "Miss Gibson?"

The Arbitor turned her head now, and her eyes opened wide. "Muffin?"

At that moment, I struck, my fist connecting with Arbitor Gibson's jaw with all the force I could muster. Her arm swung out, either in counter-attack or sheer Newtonian reaction, I cannot say, and the prongs of the motivator brushed against my chest.

Five hundred franklins of erotofluidic force surged through my body, convulsing me in an agonizing and exquisite paroxysm of pain and pleasure that I dread and crave even now as I recall it. Both of us staggered backward, then struck the ground with near simultaneity. My vision contracted to a point, then blackness.

I think it was only a few seconds later when I raised my head. Dewey was still standing by the bed, wringing his hands in consternation. Weaver was crouched by Arbitor Gibson, gently fanning her brow with a look of the greatest concern upon his face. It hurt to breathe, it hurt to sit up, it hurt to speak, and my knuckles throbbed as if I had put my hand through a mangle.

∽

"Dewey," said Weaver, "go to the innkeeper and get some ice for Miss Gibson's jaw—it's already starting to swell. And you'd best take this," he handed Dewey the motivator. "Apparently our pugilists can't be trusted with it."

"Muffin," Arbitor Gibson groaned from the floor, "it is you, isn't it?"

"It is, Miss Gibson," Weaver said, "I thought I'd never see you again."

I sat up. My head throbbed as if in a vice. "What the—" It hurt to speak. "What the devil is going on?"

"Miss Gibson enlisted and trained me," Weaver said. "I loved her from the moment I saw her. And she... she felt something for me, as well."

"I sent him away," Gibson said, with a tenderness in her voice of which I would not have thought her capable. "I had to—an arbitor can't have feelings of that sort for a compulsory. It... compromises one."

Weaver looked down at the woman who had enslaved him for three years. "But not a day has gone by since when I haven't thought of you, my dear, dear Miss Gibson."

She drew a great shuddering breath. "Nor I you, Muffin," she confessed.

"Muffin?" I said, incredulous.

Weaver smiled wryly. "It wasn't my choice, I assure you, my dear fellow."

"You are allied with... Dalrymple?" Gibson asked Weaver, investing my name with all the warm regard one might apply to a Bonaparte or a Cromwell.

"I am," Weaver affirmed. "He is a sound fellow, and a brilliant engineer."

"What of his ontological bomb, then?"

"Bomb?" Weaver and I said, in unison."

"His so-called 'threshing machine' for which he had the gall to attempt to borrow a replacement part from me."

This charge rather got my dander up. "And if you'd had the common courtesy to provide it, none of this mess would have happened!"

"Then you deny that you used that infernal engine to create the Howland Effect currently threatening the village?"

"I... I..." I stammered.

"Willa," Weaver put in, "That... thing was a terrible accident. Victor didn't even know about it until yesterday. I was there when he found out, and I swear to you that it was no act."

"Even so," she protested, "the culpability is his. He must be brought to justice!"

"If that is more important to you than stopping this thing, I shan't stop you—"

("You shan't?" I put in.

"Hush!" he demanded.)

"—I shan't stop you. But Victor is the only man in the world who might be able to prevent the coming catastrophe. Of that I am certain."

Gibson looked at him for a long moment. "Muffin, you have always been the most abominably troublesome subject I have ever futilely attempted to train."

He smiled mischievously. "But worth every second."

One corner of her mouth quirked up. "We shall see. What aid does your little criminal friend require?"

Chapter 9: The Return

Gibson obtained Ministry uniforms for Weaver and myself easily enough, though she insisted on women's uniforms, maintaining that violas were uncommon enough in the technologist corps as to excite unwanted attention. Weaver actually seemed more uncomfortable than myself, fidgeting constantly, plucking at his stays as if they were coated in itching-powder, and nearly tripping over his skirts every three steps.

Dewey was elated. "Home, Victor! We're going home!" he enthused, gripping my hands in his. "D'you think Uncle Daedalus is doing all right? I hope he remembered to pay the gas-man! He is so terribly unworldly sometimes. And your girls! Just think how they must be missing you."

"I'm not certain how interested they are in anyone who doesn't lactate at this stage in their lives," I demurred, though my heart had leapt at the thought of seeing them again.

"You might be able to manage it..." he said, scrutinizing my bosom appraisingly.

I shuddered and changed the subject. "You seemed happy enough here, though."

He shrugged. "I make the best of it. It has been rather a lark. But it's time to be going home—don't you feel it?"

Transporting the disassembled 'scaphe was no trivial task, even with the parts separated into three steamer trunks. (Arbitor Gibson did not volunteer to take one, and somehow no-one invited her to do so.) Gibson insisted that requisitioning an ipsekinetron for the trip would be far too conspicuous, so instead we dragged the trunks along. I started to object that surely a set of engineers dragging steamer trunks down the road a mile from town would be conspicuous as well, but Gibson's icy glare froze the words in my mouth.

As we neared the walls of the impromptu compound, the sun was setting once again over its fortifications, making the last day's terrors and reversals feel like a strange dream. Gibson brought our little caravan to a halt, clapping her hands briskly together. "Ship-shape, gentlemen. Reality notwithstanding, you must appear a disciplined team of Ministry engineers, not a ragged band of reckless troublemakers."

"A regular Henry at Agincourt," I muttered under my breath.

"Dalrymple," Gibson said tartly, "you have insights to impart to us?"

"No, Arbitor," I said.

"Well, then." She turned and strode towards the gate without another look back.

❦

We approached the gate and espied the lone guard, who stood—or, rather, leaned—in the stark blue radiance of an erotofluidic arc-lantern. Eventually we drew near enough that a faint and intermittent snoring could be heard emerging from his slack mouth.

Gibson sighed in exasperation, then cleared her throat loudly. The lictor started and sprang to attention, attempting to discreetly wipe the small trail of saliva from his chin while not looking excessively unmartial in the process.

"Arbitor Sterling and party for trebuchet maintenance," Gibson said crisply.

"O—of course," the guard said. "Let me just check you on the roster..."

Gibson nodded minutely, and he turned around to consult a fat ledger on the field table beside him. Unhurriedly, she extracted the motivator from her sleeve, turned its knob to maximum, and dug its prongs into one of the distracted guard's buttocks.

As he fell, twitching and gurgling, to the ground, she shook her head sadly. "It's merely the greatest threat humanity has ever known, why should they assign someone competent to guard it? Why, in-deed? Muffin, don't just stand there gaping like a landed trout. Make yourself useful and tie this idiot up. You did bring rope, didn't you?"

Weaver produced a length of some, and Gibson nodded in some-thing almost like approval. "Good. No undertaking ever failed from an excess of rope. That is my observation."

As Weaver set to tying the man up, Gibson went through his pock-ets and shortly located a massive iron key, with which she unlocked the gate; she gestured us through with an ironical wave.

❧

Dewey and I stepped through and stopped dead on the other side of the gate, gaping at the obscenity we had unwittingly created. It was perhaps the size of a small house, though its boundaries were difficult to make out, both because its outlines were unclear and because it seethed and swirled and pulsed incessantly. Fitful sparks of radiance illuminated its translucent shimmering mass from within like a thun-derhead. It made a faint sound: a murmuring, multi-voiced keening that seemed to dance ever on the edge of intelligible words, pleas or commands or terrible invocations. My stomach lurched to behold it, for it was neither living thing nor inanimate object, like a great malevolent bonfire without fuel, or a terrible whirlpool without water.

I looked about the compound. The ground, so verdant and idyllic a few weeks before, was now trampled and gouged by innumerable feet, engines of all kinds, and perhaps entities stranger still, generated by the terrible vortex. In one corner, the trebuchet crouched, like a sleeping ogre from a fairy tale. A few saplings still stood about, illuminated eerily by the vortex's light. I peered at what appeared to be a single fruit, bending down the branch of the nearest one, and found it to be a big toe, which twitched occasionally in apparent good health. I looked away, gorge rising in my stomach.

On the ground, a neat line of little white ovals extended from the mass in the centre to the wall. Closer scrutiny revealed them to be plover eggs, placed at regular intervals. Even as I watched, the vortex swallowed one up, and it softened and spread into some unidentifiable lump of pulsing crimson flesh, imprinted with the mangled ontological fields from one or both of us. I realized that the line was a way to track the vortex's accelerating growth.

"Do you feel it?" Dewey said beside me.

I felt so much, and so strongly, that I was uncertain as to what element he was referring. "The horror?" I asked.

In the corner of my transfixed vision, Dewey shook his head impatiently. "The call! The terrible pull of it. Like a fierce wind blowing me towards its awful centre."

"No," I confessed, "quite the contrary. I feel as if it and I were like magnetic poles. It is an effort just to stand this close to it."

"Curious..." Dewey said, but then Weaver and Gibson appeared, Weaver with the rest of the equipment, and Gibson, to my surprise, with the guard, still twitching in an uncoordinated manner, flung over one shoulder like a sack of potatoes.

"Well, what do you think of your handiwork, Dalrymple?" Gibson said as she flung the guard, none too gently, to the ground in one corner.

Rather than allow her to goad me, I opened the first of the trunks, extracted my tools, and began reassembling the Ontoscaphe Mark II.

The time that followed felt quite interminable. I had gone nearly without sleep for two days, the work we were embarked on was precise, and any error could prove profoundly dangerous; and underneath it all, the terrible sensation of the writhing, ever-growing vortex at our backs made each minute seem an hour. I found myself constantly glancing at the eastern sky, certain that dawn was about to break, bringing unwelcome witnesses to our secretive labours.

Nonetheless, when the 'scaphe was assembled, barely more than an hour had passed by Weaver's watch. I stood, and, wiping the worst of the machine oil off of my hands, assessed our plan of attack.

"Weaver," I said, "I have one more considerable favour to ask of you, and then, with any luck at all, we will be out of your hair, as the saying goes, permanently."

"My dear friend, I remain at your disposal. This is all really quite a grand adventure, don't you think?"

"No," I said.

Arbitor Gibson, who had stood coolly watching us through most of the preceding labours, interjected: "Muffin, darling, you are really a terribly soft touch. Don't you think you should let Dalrymple solve some of his own problems?"

Ignoring her discourtesy, I continued: "There is the matter of power for the 'scaphe, you see...."

"Ah," said Weaver, and then, "Oh!"

"Muffin would be delighted to lend his unique skills," Gibson put in smoothly, "in service to so worthy a cause." She rested a hand on the back of his neck. "Isn't that right, Muffin?"

Even in the Vortex's unearthly light, it was evident that Weaver was blushing furiously. "Yes... always happy to lend a hand," he said.

We hauled the Ontoscaphe into the trebuchet's sling, and then I ran the Vital Fluid cables from the 'scaphe down to a circlet which I placed atop Weaver's head. I started to shake his hand, but he pulled me into a fierce embrace. "Farewell," he said softly to me, "perhaps we shall meet again someday."

I found that the nagging unease that had so oppressed me on our walk out from the village was returning with renewed vigour. "Perhaps," I said. "I shall miss you, Alex. You have been a great friend to a fellow in need."

I extended my hand next to Gibson, and, to my faint surprise, she took it. "It's a shame," she said, with a small smile, "I really would quite have enjoyed breaking you to harness."

Dewey and I vaulted into the Ontoscaphe. I made to turn it on, but Weaver stopped me. "I almost forgot!" he called, then handed up two pairs of spectacles to me.

"What are these?" I said, scrutinizing their tinted lenses, handsome brass fittings, and snug leather straps.

"Safety goggles," he said. "I acquired them for you in Manchester. A tale such as this cannot be complete without them."

I looked at him quizzically, then shrugged. "Very well. Thank you." I passed one pair to Dewey, and we put them on.

∾

"Ready?" I called down to Weaver.

He drew breath to call back, but suddenly, Arbitor Gibson's slender hand was at his throat. He let out a little sound as his body became rigid under that slight pressure. "Ready," Gibson enunciated.

I turned on the 'scaphe, and at once it surged to life under the influence of Weaver's considerable libido. The massive bank of dials swung wildly as they began to monitor the ontological fields within and without the craft, and Dewey and I set to work adjusting the knobs and levers to align the Mark II for its maiden—and likely final—voyage.

Under the circumstances, I could spare little attention for the proceedings below us, as Arbitor Gibson played upon my friend like a

finely-tuned instrument. Clearly, she had retained a detailed recollection of Weaver's anatomy and responses, and not a touch went awry,
producing a strong and steady stream of erotofluidic force from the
very start.

Finding the headings for our destination proved absurdly easy.
The 'scaphe's instruments responded like a well-trained horse, know-
ing its path with only the lightest guidance from the riders. Something was wrong, though. As I tried to coordinate our internal field
with the jump ahead of us, the readings kept coming out wildly off.
The passage was still possible, but the path stood no chance of obvi-
ating the vortex. What was I overlooking?

I looked about. Below us, Weaver was stripped to the waist, arms
pinned behind his back, his skin a dense field of white and pink, as
Miss Gibson scored him in intricate patterns with her cruel and patient
fingernails. She crooned unintelligibly in his ear as he twitched and
writhed under her hands.

The 'scaphe itself should present no trouble—it was nearly entirely of metal and should be entirely transparent to the ontological
fields. Our clothes were new, but light and inert enough that they
could not be producing the numbers I saw. Dewey was looking anxiously at me now, aware that something was awry, but with no
inkling what.

Then I understood. In a moment, I knew what was wrong, what
I had to do.

I took a deep breath and prepared myself. "All is ready," I called
out confidently. "Countdown to activation."

"What is—?" Dewey tried to put in.

"Five!" I called out, and put out my hand for silence.

"Four!"

Dewey faced forward and braced himself against the coming
shock.

"Three!"

There was a report, Weaver cried out, and there was another surge
of erotofluidic force through the Ontoscaphe. I glanced down in time
to see Arbitor Gibson swing back with her hand and strike his face a
second time. His second cry was muffled as she leaned in to kiss him

hard on the mouth, her other hand tugging fiercely at one of Weaver's nipples.

"Two!"

I poised my hand over the activation lever.

"One!"

I pulled the lever.

As the air began to shimmer about us, I vaulted out of my seat and sprang to the ground. I landed badly and fell to my knees, one ankle a blaze of pain.

"Victor! Victor! What are you doing?" Dewey called after me.

I ignored his cries. "Fire the trebuchet!" I called to Gibson. "Now!"

Dewey attempted to follow me, but the ontological force swirling about the 'scaphe was like a solid mass now, and pressing his hand into it wedged him like a fly in tar paper.

Gibson extracted her hand from Weaver's trousers, flicked the circlet off of his brow, and took hold of the lever that operated the trebuchet. One last time, she looked quizzically at me. "Now!" I demanded once more. The Ontoscaphe was beginning to show flickers of translucence as its presence in this ontosphere was compromised by the fields it was superimposing on itself.

Gibson pulled the lever, and, with a mighty lurch, the trebuchet flung its load into the heart of the vortex. The Ontoscaphe disappeared from view into the swirling murk, and there was a moment's quiet, the only sound being the continued eerie wail the vortex generated.

Then, without so much as a pop, it was gone, with no obstacle but a few transformed plover's eggs between ourselves and the far wall.

In a moment, Weaver, shirtless, trousers unfastened, was at my side. "What the devil did you do that for?" he demanded.

I shook my head ruefully. "I'm not the man I once was," I said.

"What on earth do you—" then comprehension began to dawn in his face. "Oh," he said.

"Well, I still don't see what all this madness was about," Gibson said, standing over us with a disapproving frown.

"To burst the vortex," I explained to her, standing carefully and testing my throbbing ankle, "we needed to penetrate it with a concentrated dose of the ontological fields that had generated it. Anything else would simply have fuelled its strength, but Dewey by himself could puncture its integrity, so that it ruptured like a burst soap-bubble. My field isn't the same as it was when I arrived. I'm still female."

"So you——?"

"Couldn't go back. Not yet, at any rate. Once I'm male again, it shouldn't be too difficult to go through without doing any damage. But until then, I daren't risk it."

"How long will that be?"

"Days. Months. Years. Never. Ontology is not yet an exact science," I said with a sigh.

"Well, then!" Gibson put in, with a smile of grim satisfaction. "You shall have your opportunity to pay your debt to society, after all."

Weaver turned to the arbitor, and his cheeks, which had paled in the drama of the preceding minutes, flushed once more with hot emotion. "Willa, if you turn this brave, good man in to the authorities like a criminal, after all he has done to make this right, I shall never forgive you."

Gibson blinked slowly, a look of almost comical dismay upon her visage. It was evident that, having found Weaver once more after years of separation, the prospect of losing him immediately filled her with dread. "If you vouch for his good character, Muffin, then that is sufficient for me," she said at last, though it clearly pained her to do so.

Weaver smiled broadly and embraced her. "Oh, Willa, I knew you were better-hearted than that."

Then he stepped back, and, after a moment of gathering his resolve, he spoke once more: "Miss Gibson, will you marry me?"

"Muffin, sweet Muffin, you know I am married to the Ministry."

"Leave it! Elope with me!"

"Oh, Muffin," Gibson sighed, in a quite uncharacteristic agony of indecision.

"If you will only be mine, my wife, my cruel taskmistress, I shall be quite the happiest man in all the Empire."

"Yes!" she cried, and she seemed to rise in stature as resolution filled her once more. "I shall be yours, and you shall scream for mercy."

They embraced.

◦◦◦

We left the empty trunks and the tools in the compound. The guard, we figured, would be found and untied in little enough time.

Weaver and Gibson took turns supporting me on the long and painful walk back to town; once in my room, I slept through the day and through the night, awakening late the following morning.

"We elope this very day," Weaver told me over breakfast and massive quantities of strong, hot tea. "We intend to see the world, and we may not be back for quite some time."

"I wish the both of you the very greatest happiness," I told him sincerely. "May your adventures be both numerous and tame."

Weaver smiled at this. "The former I think I can guarantee. What of yourself? What are your plans now?"

I looked down at my teacup. "That remains to be seen. I may be here for quite some time, so I'd best go about making the best of it. In this sphere, I am both homeless and friendless, so I shall have to rely on my wits and my charming manners to get by."

"You are neither," Weaver admonished me. "You left Manchester an honorary Joanite. You will return to that city a full brother, with all the resources of that society to draw upon." He drew a heavy ring off of one finger and handed it to me. "Your own seal will be made up shortly, but in the meantime, here is mine. You were right when we first met, and I was wrong. You have indeed become a viola. Now I must go—my bride awaits me. But we shall meet again."

Once more he embraced me, and then left.

◦◦◦

The Brotherhood of St. Joan did indeed welcome me with open arms. Even Walter Purslaine seemed pleased to see me in my new form. My ontological research has not terminated here, though I have perhaps proceeded with greater caution than before.

If all has gone well, this manuscript may be, in many parts, redundant with what Dewey has already told you in person. But if some disaster has befallen him, this may be the first news you receive of his fate, and mine. The enclosed diagrams contain my design for an ontograph machine, whereby sheets of paper may be conveyed from one ontosphere to another, with no risk at either end. Daedalus should be happy to build you one to these specifications, and that should allow your correspondence to reach me, just as, God willing, this document has reached you.

In the eyes of the world, a widow you must be, my dear Eleanor, and I commend you to seek your pleasures where you will; indeed, I would mourn not just for you, but for all mankind, were your charms to be withheld forever from all of my unworthy brethren.

Nonetheless, not worlds, nor more than worlds, can sunder us entirely. And one day I retain hope that I may return to you. But until such a time, I remain,

Your, late, loving husband,
Victor

The Cyclopaedia Erotofluidica
(Glossary)

To some readers, a few of the terms used in *The Erotofluidic Age* may be unfamiliar. A selection of these are defined below.

Arbitor: A person empowered by the Ministry of Erotofluidics to test, select, and train Compulsories (q.v.).

Butch: A young man who sells snacks on a locomotive car. So-called because they aprons they wear resemble those of butchers.

Compulsory: A citizen of the British Empire engaged in compulsory service to the Ministry of Erotofluidics. Only those with a high aptitude for the distinctive labour required are invited to serve. The term of service is three years.

Daguerrotype machine: An early type of camera.

Erotofluidic: Pertaining to the vital fluids (q.v.) exuded by a person in a state of sexual excitement. Also the science, art, and technology of extracting and harnessing said fluids.

French letter: Condom.

Gamahuche: The act of cunnilingus.

Geoduck: A type of large surf-clam distinctive to the Pacific Northwest of North America, distinguished primarily by its massive siphon.

Godemiche: Dildo.

Ipsekinetron: An erotofluidically-powered horseless carriage.

Motivator: a device similar in theory and operation to a cattle-prod, but employing erotofluidic (q.v.) force rather than electrical charge.

Ontology: The study of the categories to which all things belong. An ontological engine would be a device able to directly manipulate those categories; the question of whether such an engine is indeed possible is hotly debated in the field.

Scrimshandry: The art of carving ivory.

Terminando: A touring event whereat an Arbitor (q.v.) tests and selects candidates for compulsory service (q.v.).

Thermionic valve: Vacuum tube.

Trebuchet: A lesser-known sibling of the catapult, using a counterweight rather than elastic tension.

Velocipede: Bicycle, esp. of the chainless "penny-farthing" type.

Viola: A person who, ------- ------ ---- ---- ------, ------ -- ---- -- - ---.

Vital fluids: Any of the subtle energies exuded by living things in varying degrees. Humans, as the crown of Creation, possess the greatest capacity for vital fluid generation.

About the Author

Vinnie Tesla has worked (or at least drawn a paycheck) as a whitewater guide, information architect, bicycle deliveryman (by, not of), porn video reviewer, and desktop publisher.

His purchase, in adolescence, of a mass-market paperback of *The Pearl* was undoubtedly the pivotal event that turned him towards his calling as a fake Victorian pornographer. His subsequent internship at Circlet Press was just the icing on the cake.

He has an intermittent blog at journal.vinnietesla.com and a bunch of free fiction online at vinnietesla.com/stories, including Victim/Victorian, the pornographic novella to which *The Erotofluidic Age* is a prequel.

He lives in Massachusetts with his spousalbeast.

"The Ontological Engine" is also available as an audiobook, read by the author.

Acknowledgements

This book owes a great many debts to sources of influence, inspiration, and support. The several anonymous authors of The Pearl must always come first. They took serious risks to share their silly, flimsy, but somehow compelling and memorable sexual fantasies with posterity. My debt to Mary Shelly's vision, and to William Gilbert, P.G. Wodehouse, and Arthur Conan Doyle's language is similarly great, though I shudder to think what any of those great writers would think of the work they influenced.

Cecilia Tan has been an inspiration, and occasionally a mentor, to me. Circlet editors Lauren Burka and Jen Levine have been meticulous, appreciative, and diligent supports.

Balan Nusnubilis, PhD, has been a rich source of data about the love lives of sessile bivalves. My mother has been an invaluable source of information and research about several aspects of Victorian language and culture, despite having been strictly forbidden to read this book.

Finally, and mostly, my amazing spousalbeast has been my most inspiring muse, my most sensitive editor, and my most stalwart support throughout the whole process. In a list of indispensables, she is the indispensablest.

"The Ontological Engine" was previously published in *Up For Grabs*, edited by Lauren P. Burka, a publication of Circlet Press, Inc.

www.ingramcontent.com/pod-product-compliance
Lightning Source LLC
Chambersburg PA
CBHW030225180626
46810CB00008B/2969